OPENINGS

OPENINGS

Thirteen Stories

LUCY CALDWELL

faber

First published in 2024
by Faber & Faber Limited
The Bindery, 51 Hatton Garden
London EC1N 8HN

Typeset by Typo•glyphix, Burton-on-Trent DE14 3HE
Printed and bound in the UK by CPI Group (UK) Ltd, Croydon CR0 4YY

'The Counting Sheep' and 'Daphne' were first broadcast by
BBC Radio 4 – July 2021 and June 2023 respectively.

'Lay Me Down' was first published in the *Irish Times* magazine
in December 2022.

'Dark Matters' was first published in *Collision: Stories from
the Science of CERN* (Comma Press, 2023).

Extract from *Three Sisters* by Anton Chekhov, translation © Elisaveta Fen, 1951.
Published by Penguin Books. Used with permission

A CIP record for this book
is available from the British Library

ISBN 978–0–571–382750

MIX
Paper | Supporting
responsible forestry
FSC® C171272

Printed and bound in the UK on FSC® certified paper in line with our continuing
commitment to ethical business practices, sustainability and the environment.
For further information see faber.co.uk/environmental-policy

2 4 6 8 10 9 7 5 3

for my Tom

I think a human being has got to have some faith, or at least he's got to seek faith. Otherwise his life will be empty, empty . . . How can you live and not know why the cranes fly, why children are born, why the stars shine in the sky! . . . You must either know why you live, or else . . . nothing matters . . . everything's just wild grass . . .

Anton Chekhov,
Three Sisters (trans. Elisaveta Fen)

Contents

OPENINGS

If You Lived Here You'd Be Home By Now

MY MOTHER WAS DYING, SO I GOT A KITTEN. Logistically, it made no sense: it would just make everything harder, when or if I was able to travel to see her. It was a sort of helplessness, I suppose – she was so far away. Also, she hated cats. She always said she hated the way you could feel their bones moving under their skin. It felt worth it even just to revive that joke on the family group – to have something else to say.

The kitten was our neighbour's cat's, from a few doors down. During the first weeks of lockdown, working from the back bedroom, I'd watch her make her daily rounds along the walls and fences of our terrace's back gardens. In the afternoons she'd sunbathe, moving from one shed or rooftop to another as the sun swung round, coming to my kitchen roof in the late afternoon, when it had its turn in the pouring westerly light. The back bedroom got very stuffy: often when I opened the window she'd jump up and come in, delicately, a paw at a time over the windowsill, green eyes bold. We suspected the tenants before us had fed her, she was so at home in our house.

She'd inspect each room, tail twitching, then settle down on the landing at the top of the stairs, purring like an engine when the girls stroked her. It became part of the rhythm of those days, and when our neighbours said Bella would be having a litter soon, and were we interested, to the girls' delight I said yes straight away, despite the fact that we'd never had a pet before, despite the clause in our tenancy agreement forbidding it – despite everything.

We collected the kitten – a black-and-white male – on the day it turned eight weeks. Our neighbour scooped it into our new cat-carrier and handed it over, and that was that, we suddenly had a cat. I took a picture of the girls beaming, holding up the carrier, and sent it to my family group, which was me, my sister, my sister's husband and our mum. It was lunchtime with me which meant bedtime in Sydney – there wouldn't be a response for hours, unless my mum was up in the night. The drugs she was on made sleep unpredictable – but the sleeping pills she took in the hope of countering that meant the midnight messages she sent were often unintelligible. There'd be a garbled string of capital letters, autocorrected words and arbitrary emojis, and I'd have to wait until my sister woke and chimed in to be sure they hadn't been my mum's last words. To caption the photo, I wrote *Another reason to be grateful you can't visit!* It horrified my sister's husband, the way we talked to each other: he just didn't get it. For his sake, or maybe for the opposite reason, because I still half-resented him being in our family group, I added the emoji of the laughing-crying cat.

2

Mum had always wanted to move back to Australia – she said they talked about Coogee, with its wide sandy beaches, its salt-water pools cut into the headland. Its snorkelling trails, its surfing – the laid-back teenage years she wanted us to have, and all just a short ride into Sydney. But when my father died, everyone told her not to make any major life decisions for a year, and when the year was up I was sitting the eleven-plus and starting secondary school, and then my sister was, and we didn't want to emigrate. At least, she says we didn't: I don't remember being asked. I think I would have liked it. I sometimes still wonder who I might have been, this surfer version of myself.

In the end it was my sister who went back – or, from her point of view, went. She and her English boyfriend, first of all on working-holiday visas, and then when they settled there, got full citizenship, had the twins, Mum went out to visit more and more frequently, the only family – the only child-care – they had, and they convinced her to make it permanent. Coogee, in fact most of the coastal suburbs of Sydney, were too expensive by then, and so they'd all settled in a town called Coffs Harbour, a few hours north of Sydney on the Pacific Highway, where they had condos in the same low-rise building. When my mum was a child, there had been a big banana statue in Coffs Harbour, and little else. Now there was a whole Big Banana Fun Park, with water slides, laser tag, mini-golf – even an opal centre where you could watch geodes being split and rough-cut, and buy opal jewellery.

I hadn't yet been to visit them. Pregnancy complications, the terror of something happening to my daughter's lungs at 35,000 feet – there'd always been some reason to put off going until a better time, and now I couldn't. It was a strange, vertiginous feeling, that you were on the other side of the world: as if the map, instead of announcing *You are here*, had an arrow saying *They are there*.

We took the cat-carrier into the kitchen, set it down on the floor and carefully unzipped it. The kitten was cowering at the very back, pressed as small as it could make itself, a cloudy ball of paws and tail. The advice we'd read online was to let it come out in its own time, and to confine it to one room for the first few days. My younger daughter jumped around describing all its new things – its food and water bowls, its litter tray, cat tree and scratching post, cushioned basket. My elder daughter dangled a catnip mouse and a fishing-rod toy at it, but the kitten didn't move. They laid a trail of cat treats leading out from the carrier, but it wasn't interested in those either. After a while, they got bored and went off to do something else.

I stayed crouched down on my hunkers, trying to talk to it in a soothing voice. Then Bella appeared on the fence, mewing.

'Bella's here!' the girls yelled, and ran to the back door to let her in.

'No, wait!' I guldered back.

We couldn't keep letting her in now that we had her kitten, I explained to them: this had to become his territory, not hers.

They stopped, frowned. 'But she always comes in.'

'She can't,' I said. 'Not any more.'

On the fence, Bella miaowed. She could see us through the window – she knew we could see her. I pulled the blind down, switched on the radio – but the kitten had already heard her too. It was sitting upright, quivering, as if a current was running right from its ears to its tail. Bella miaowed again, louder. The kitten mewled, the most piteous sound – then darted out of the carrier, bolted in a panic around the kitchen, this way and that, hissing as we yelped and tried not to step on it, and finally squeezed through a tiny gap in the kickboard behind the kitchen units and the sink.

I'd had a pest control man tell me that a mouse can get through a gap no bigger than a biro – but I wouldn't have believed a kitten could fit through a space the size of a mousehole.

'Topsy!' my youngest daughter shrieked.

'He's not called Topsy,' barked the elder. 'Topsy was if we got a girl kitten, he's a boy. Shadow,' she shouted. 'Shadow!'

'Shadow was if we got the black one. It's not fair if you get to choose the name. Mummy, it's not fair!'

'Both of you, please.'

'Is the kitten stuck in there?'

'Of course not,' I said, with more confidence than I felt.

'But how are you going to get him out, Mummy?'

'Shall we phone the fire brigade?'

'Not yet,' I said. 'Let's just see what happens.'

Bella was miaowing, plaintive, insistent, and under the kickboard her kitten had started to cry back to her, a desperate wail.

'Please can we let her in,' my eldest said, looking on the verge of tears now herself. 'The kitten wants her.'

'The kitten has to learn he's our kitten now,' I said.

For two awful hours, Bella and her kitten called to each other, before eventually he went silent, and she left.

'She was probably just singing him a lullaby,' I said to the girls. But the pitch of the animals' distress had been so evident they both just looked at me. Their faces were blotchy with their own distress and tears.

'I don't like having a kitten,' the youngest said, burrowing her face into me, and the elder said, 'I don't want to, Mummy, but I think maybe we should give him back.'

'Look,' I said, 'the first night was always going to be tricky. I promise it will be better in the morning.'

The kitten hid all afternoon, all evening. It was almost ten o'clock before I finally got the girls to sleep, cuddled up in the same bunk bed, and went downstairs to see if there was any sign of him yet.

There wasn't. Not a single treat, not a scrap of food had gone. Online, I found a thread on a pet forum about a new kitten who'd hidden inside a TV cabinet for five days, coming out only at night to eat and drink and use the litter tray; another person chimed in to say that their kitten had made a home for the first few days *inside* a sofa. I felt a bit better then. I moved the food and water bowls closer to the kitchen unit. I sat as still as I could, and listened. There wasn't so much as a peep. Kittens slept a lot, I'd read that – it had probably just exhausted itself. It would come out when it was hungry: it had to. There was nothing for it under there.

And then I thought, with a nasty jolt, that there were actually bait boxes behind the sink full of rodent poison – the mouse man had left them there. I had to get the kitten out. I gave the edge of the kickboard a tug, but it seemed fixed onto the unit, and I didn't want to yank too hard in case part of the unit collapsed. The mouse man had dismantled the whole row of units when he was here, in order to fill up any holes in the plumbing with expanding foam.

In a panic, I called my husband.

'Is it your mum?' he said.

'What? No – no, it's the new kitten. It's stuck behind the kickboard and won't come out.'

'Right,' he said. 'Sweetheart—'

'I know,' I said. 'I know we, I, shouldn't have gotten it, I know it will just make things more difficult. I know that we can't ask your sister to take it because of her allergies and I know that catteries are horrible, stressful places. I know it would have been better to wait and get a kitten in a few months' time or next year, if we still wanted one then. I know,' I said. 'I know I shouldn't have called you about something so trivial. I know there's nothing you can do. I don't know what to do,' I said. 'I don't know what to do.'

He sighed, started to say something, stopped. 'Oh, sweetheart,' he said.

For a moment, we just breathed together.

He was only in hospital digs that night because he was in the middle of a particularly brutal nursing rota, staff shortages, nights. But somehow we were instantly back in those early days of lockdown, when we might as well have been calling each other from different time zones in different hemispheres. The space opened up again so easily I wondered if it would always be there, now, between us – all the things, the experiences, that were essentially uncommunicable. We'd both been so terrified, initially, for what the virus might mean for our youngest daughter, who'd been on a ventilator for several weeks after birth, who still saw a respiratory consultant for annual check-ups, that he'd moved to hospital accommodation to protect us, and stayed there for the first nine weeks. He hadn't been part of us, our little routines – the ways we merged. The girls had both ended up sleeping in my bed, and something about the sustained physical proximity had regressed us all to a more primitive state, where we seemed to feel each other's emotions, a few times even seemed to dream each other's dreams. We'd done random things for hours, like follow YouTube tutorials to braid each other's hair, or make dozens of origami cranes, or set up a tattoo parlour with a pack of water transfers I found, things that seemed trivial when we related them on FaceTime calls, as if it was only playing.

He cleared his throat.

'I'm going to have to go back in,' he said, 'but I'm sure it will all be fine.'

'I'm sorry,' I said. 'I shouldn't have called.'

'You know I'll always answer,' he said. 'And if I can't speak straight away, I'll call you back as soon as I can.'

'I know.'

'Here, do you have a name for it?' he said.

I felt a rush of love for him – for the ways he was trying.

'Not yet,' I said.

It was 7 a.m. in Sydney. My sister's husband, and almost simultaneously my sister, read my message. He didn't reply, but my sister wrote *I hope you can't feel its wee bones moving under its skin!!* with a string of the laughing-crying cat faces. 8 a.m., 8.30: my sister always dropped in on our mum on her way to work. Sure enough, 8.40 their-time, my phone registered that Mum had seen the messages. A moment later, *A cat?* she wrote. *You have not, have you???* And then a third: *Well you know this means I'm NOT EVER coming round yours!!!*

After that I watched her *typing* . . . for almost ten minutes, after which a message came through that filled the whole screen. It was about our dad's granny, who'd apparently hated cats so much she'd hoke out the smallest potatoes from the bag and keep them in a basin by the back door, ready to fire at any neighbourhood cats who set foot in her garden. As a result she'd had potato plants sprouting up here, there and everywhere, in the randomest of places.

I hadn't known that story. It would have taken it out of Mum, concentrating on writing a message for that long. She'd been doing it more and more recently; anecdotes, memories. I screenshotted the message, because I wanted to remember it but knew I wouldn't be able to go back through the family thread.

I messaged her privately then. *How are you doing anyway, Mum? xo*

Ah you know, she said. A moment later, my phone started buzzing, and my own face loomed up on it – it took a moment to realise that my mum was trying to FaceTime me. I was appalled at how old I looked, how unkempt – my hair going every which way, and in the light it looked even greyer than it actually was at the temples. I'd last seen her two years ago, and I hadn't been grey at all. I quickly tried to move to a more flattering angle, more forgiving light. Maybe it was just vanity, but I couldn't bear my mum seeing me looking so old. By then the call had cut out, so I FaceTimed back. Mum's face when she answered looked surprised to see me.

'You FaceTimed me,' I said.

'No, you just FaceTimed me.'

'No, before that.'

'Oh,' she said. 'I didn't mean to. It must have been an accident.' She frowned and held the phone out at arm's length to study it. She was in her medical-grade bed, wearing a Ramones t-shirt. They played the likes of 'Roll Out the Barrel' and 'We'll Meet Again' in old people's homes now, my sister had told me, when they really should have been playing punk.

'I'll FaceTime you your-tonight my-tomorrow with the girls,' I said. 'They'd love to see you.' That was a lie: they were shy of Granny Marge, now that they knew she was dying, and they had to be bribed to say anything at all, carefully steered not to say the wrong thing.

'Well, that cat had better not put in an appearance, is all I'm saying!'

'Ha!'

'Where is it, anyway? You couldn't see anything of it in that picture you sent. Was there really a cat in there or were you just pulling my leg?'

'There was a cat. There is a cat. It's hiding.'

Mum pretended to shudder. I pretended to laugh.

'Well, I'm going to have to love you and leave you, possum,' she said. 'The first nurse comes at nine, that's any minute now.'

'Ok, Mum. You take care—' But she'd already gone.

Bella was back on the fence again. I could hear her thin, persistent call. I waited for a scuffle and answering mew from under the units, but – nothing.

Bella called and called. The pitch of her calls rose until it was almost unbearable. The kitten didn't answer.

Finally, she turned and left again, back to her other kittens, the hold they still had on her.

I was certain of it now: our kitten was dead.

It was past midnight, too late to knock on anyone's door, or to start hacking at the units myself. I could get up early to try to do it, and to dispose of the kitten's body, but no doubt the girls would wake early too, and they'd be there for the full horror of it, a helpless creature failed, dead of terror, or heartbreak – or my incompetence. There'd been a thing one of the baby books had said, for those days that you felt you'd done nothing, not even managed to dress properly or to shower: you should remind yourself that you'd gotten both yourself and another living creature through. And I hadn't. There wasn't a hope of sleeping. I could still feel Bella's, still feel the kitten's, distress. I'd absorbed as much of it as I could into my own body, I thought, so that my girls would feel less of it. I could actually feel it humming in me, like a sort of toxin. It was what mothers did, but it couldn't be good for you. My sister had used the word *riddled* with Mum, when she'd told me: that's how the phrase went, *she's riddled with it*. Riddled, as if it were a puzzle, to which there was an answer, that would make sense of this, of everything.

I could feel my mind racing, the sort of thoughts that make a treacherous half-sense that's no sense at all. If I lay in bed, the thoughts would persist; I would lose the run of myself. I went into my study, clambered over the desk and through the window onto the roof.

To my surprise, my neighbour to the left was on the roof of her kitchen too. We both used to do it during lockdown, but I hadn't for a while, and she looked too pregnant to be climbing through windows and onto rooftops.

'Hiya,' she whisper-called across.

'How're you doing,' I whisper-called back.

'What are you at?'

'Couldn't sleep. You?'

'Same,' she said. 'Though I should be doing everything to get it while I can.'

'There can't be long now,' I said.

'Nope. Any day. Can't come soon enough, this wain, I'm telling you.'

She was the same age as me, more or less, and the baby was her second. The funny thing was, her firstborn was also pregnant with *her* first child – the two babies were due to be born this summer, within a couple of weeks of each other. My neighbour had had her daughter at sixteen, and her daughter had had a whole life, school, university, PGCE, first teaching job, gotten engaged to be married, pregnant, and now her baby was going to be older than its aunt or uncle, her half-sister or brother the same age as her mother's first grandchild. My neighbour thought it was hilarious. Her daughter had always been very sensible and hard-working, she said; like so many of her gener-ation barely touched a drop of alcohol, let alone drugs. We'd had a sort of pantomime going in lockdown:

whenever she saw me, she mimed rolling a huge joint, lighting it, and passing it over. I'd mime reaching to take it and we'd exhale in euphoric unison. She rolled and passed the pretend joint now, and I took it.

'Thanks,' I said, taking a huge imaginary toke. 'I needed that.'

'How come?'

I told her about Bella and the kitten and she said that was what had woken her, right enough – the yowling of that cat on the fence.

'It even set Loki off,' she said, 'and he's normally pretty chilled.'

'Sorry,' I said. But even as I said it, Bella was stalking along the fence, already beginning to miaow. 'Here we go again,' I said, feeling sick. 'I am so sorry.'

'Why do you not just let her in?' my neighbour said. 'If she's used to coming in – if her kitten's inside – why not just let her in?'

'I thought it would make it harder for them,' I said, 'that a clean break would be easier in the long run?'

'Harder for all of us if this keeps up,' she said. 'Jeez, honey – are you crying?'

The shame of it – I'd hoped it would be too dark for her to see.

'I'm pretty sure the kitten's dead,' I said. 'It hasn't touched any food or water the whole time it's been here – and there hasn't been so much as a peep from it in hours.'

'Probably just in shock. Let the mother-cat in. Here, wait on me, I'll come round and we'll do it together.' She hoisted herself up and climbed slowly back through her window; I wiped my face, and took a breath, and did the same. I waited for her at the front door, and together we went through and opened the back door. Bella leapt down and in, and without pausing to scrabble and claw at the laundry basket, or do any of the things she usually did, she went straight for the hole in the kickboard and started to make a low chirruping noise.

And then – the miracle. Through the impossible gap came the little kitten, first a paw, then a head, then all of him. He shook his head, twitched his tail, leapt up and nestled into Bella, and she chirruped and groomed him, and he chirruped back and mewed and jumped at her, batting at her face, and the two of them started flowing round the kitchen together while I watched in a disbelief that felt close to joy.

My neighbour, more practically minded, busied about stuffing up the hole with tea towels. Bella and the kitten went to the food bowls, the litter tray, the scratching post, the cat basket, as if she was inspecting his new living quarters, all the while making the extraordinary low chirrup.

'What do I do when she wants to leave?' I said, and my neighbour shrugged.

'Just let her leave. They'll get used to it. It might even be a good thing in the end, him seeing she's comfortable here – might make him come out of himself a wee bit easier. But just for God's sake don't make any of us put up with that awful yowling.'

'I seriously can't thank you enough.'

'Sure, what have I done? I just know cats.'

After she'd gone, I sat for a while on the kitchen floor, watching Bella and the kitten. They were so happy together. I thought it must be what heaven was like – a reunion, against all the odds, the seeing and holding and feeling and breathing-in of a loved one, let go or given up or lost. I thought of the strange shy wonder of seeing my husband again, when those nine interminable weeks were passed, and it seemed we had been spared. How solid he'd felt – how warm and real. The way the girls had touched him, laughing, as if to touch him was an outrageous thing, and the way they'd run and hidden from him, and let him find them and tickle them until they couldn't breathe. The way we'd all piled onto the sofa and clung to each other. The nine weeks had seemed an age, and they were; they were their own eternity of sorts. But they had passed. My dad had been a humanist – he'd said there was nothing else but us, here, now, and the dignity and respect we must accord each other. Mum reminded us of that, every year on his anniversary. For that to be the case you had to believe that this was all there was. But what if there was a way of thinking of death as a sort of separation that was just an illusion of separation – something we were meant to understand on a metaphysical level, but were here to experience in a material way, here now through these bodies — like this? A way of thinking about time as not a lens through which to see, but as a sort of miasm — that we entered, trepidatiously maybe, but willingly, somewhere, somehow, before all this, in order to better understand?

For a moment, I seemed to come fleetingly close to an almost-understanding. Or maybe it was just more untethered midnight thinking that would cease to mean anything come morning.

What time was it in Sydney? It took barely a second to make the calculation; the world clock lodged in my solar plexus.

Despite all that had happened in it, barely an hour had passed. By my mum's 10 a.m., the first nurse would be gone, and she would be dozing, maybe, as she found the care visits exhausting. Dozing, making the most of the fresh influx of painkilling drugs. There was a little plastic case my sister had been given that had enough morphine to ease any suffering that got untenable, as they had carefully put it. The hope was she wouldn't need it for weeks. I had a British passport by dint of my birth, and an Irish passport through my dad, and I'd never seen the need to follow up on my entitlement to Australian citizenship before. But the papers were in the system now, and if they came through in time, as a passport holder I could go there, if I could get the flights, though it would mean a two-week hotel quarantine. It would be the longest I'd ever been without the girls — I'd never, in fact, left both of them for more than a night — and yet I wondered how, once there, I could ever leave again. What the least-worst-case scenario might be. Was it worse for my girls for me to be gone, or for me to be here but not-here? Was it worse for my mum to leave me, or for me to leave her?

We're each other's home, Mum had often said after Dad died, but that wasn't quite it, or it wasn't quite all. After all, it was what they had always said to each other too. Home couldn't be other people, much as we might want it to be.

I thought suddenly of the sign on the way back from the airport when we were little – a billboard advertising a new housing estate, built in what was otherwise the back end of nowhere. *If you lived here*, it said, *you'd be home by now!* and my sister and I had thought it the cleverest thing. 'If we lived here,' both of us would start to chant as we neared the new estate, 'Dad, Mum, Mum! If we lived here . . .' and the four of us would finish in a gulder, 'we'd be home by now!'

Bella was getting restless – going to the door, pawing at it. In a moment, I'd have to get up and put her out, and hope the kitten was ok. And then I'd try to find a way of texting the memory of the billboard to my family group, in a way that was joking enough for them to be able to respond with emojis of laughter.

Fiction

YOU APPLIED FOR THE FESTIVAL'S BURSARY, BUT DIDN'T WIN. Your mum was disappointed for you – more disappointed than you were yourself – and she offered to pay, insisted on paying, and after a while it was easier to be grateful than to refuse.

She lives alone now, since you went to uni. Two days a week she volunteers at a charity shop, on Tuesday nights she does French classes, Thursdays Pilates. You don't know what she does at the weekend.

Your mum asks about the writer leading the workshop; if his work is good. You tell her it is. You don't tell her you sort of read it more wanting to than *actually* liking it. There is one good story in his first collection, the sort you can instantly tell is properly good, about a young boy abused by an elderly family member. But none of the rest of the stories – what is it, you think, and how, how does it work? – quite feel the same.

The workshop runs for the five days of the festival, from nine till midday, in a secondary school on the edge of the town. You're still not that long out of school yourself, but even the middle-aged women joke that it gives them the willies, walking the echoing corridors past the staff room.

There are eight of you in the workshop, just over half its capacity: the five middle-aged women, two retired men, and you're by far the youngest. You go round one by one, introducing yourselves. Most of the others have done workshops before at other festivals: they set out what they hope to get from the week, and him. There are bursts of raucous laughter from the classroom next door where a younger writer, recently shortlisted for a clatter of major awards, is leading a sold-out course on the novel. You watch as your writer shuffles then drops his photocopies, runs a hand through hair which is thinning, clears his throat. He's older than his author picture in the brochure. When he looks up, you try to smile encouragingly.

When he asks questions, you make yourself answer them, though you've never been the sort to speak up in class. You volunteer to read aloud from the story he hands around. You even ask a question about his own work, to show that you've read it. He asked to read work from participants ahead of the workshop, and you agonised over what to send through: your best two stories, or were they too similar, and should you show range instead, or maybe the thing you'd most recently written, though it still seemed unfinished, in case he could help? The festival administrator said, Just send what you're happiest with, and so, in the end, you'd emailed her the two best. But he doesn't refer to them, gives no indication, in fact, that he's read any of your work. One of the retired men is writing his memoirs. The other a historical biography. Two of the women couldn't get onto the novel course, though it's novels they're working on, and the other three are in a book club together and decided to give writing a go. You don't think, from the exercises he sets that you read out in class, that any of them is particularly good, but then again, it's hard to tell; it all seems so artificial, and not what real writing – whatever that might be – is all about.

You text your mum daily updates with exclamation marks.

After the final session, you all go to the pub, and after a couple of rounds he ends up sitting next to you. We haven't discussed your writing, he says. We should discuss your writing.

Ok, you say. Ok. You push your half-pint of lager-and-lime away, reach in your bag for your notebook.

He lays a hand on your bag.

Not here, he says. Somewhere more quiet. I've got a

thing at five, but what about after that, say six thirty, seven?

It's the closing night of the festival and there's an event with a writer you don't want to miss. But you also don't want to pass up this chance.

Thank you, you say, that's so kind of you, thank you so much. Whenever suits best.

Great, he says. Well, why don't we make it dinner?

Oh, you say, ok, and he says, Great, again, and names the place.

Your mum has texted wanting to know how the last day's gone. You know you should call her, but you want to wait till you know what he thinks of your stories. You know too she'll ask about the others on the course, why they're not going for dinner. You wonder again if any of them heard him suggest it, and whether they minded.

Instead you text back it's been brilliant, exclamation marks, and promise to call her tomorrow, from the train station.

Back in the hotel you wash your face and restraighten your hair, but you keep the same clothes on so you don't look dressed up, and you don't put on make-up, not even bronzer: you want to look serious, intellectual. Then you read and reread the two stories you gave him, until it's time to go.

You're early and he's late. You sit there long enough to start wondering what you're doing. One of the retired men from your workshop walks past, holding hands with his wife, and they stop at the door and look at the menu and you wonder if they're going to come in, and what you'll say if they do, but after a while they walk on. Eventually, in he blusters, battered satchel, festival tote bag, books under his arm, so obviously unembarrassed that you relax a bit too. The restaurant is modern, brightly lit; there are people on their own as well as couples, one table of friends. It's seven o'clock: why wouldn't you have dinner? It's just a normal, practical thing to do. The writer talks – about panels he's been on, about audience members who wouldn't stop talking, moderators who got the title of his second book wrong. You smile, nod. He seems to have forgotten he's not talking to another writer, a real writer. Here you are, talking writing with a writer at a festival, over dinner, no big deal. This is it, you think, what it's like, this thing you've wanted for so very long, this world behind the curtain.

When the waitress comes you order risotto, in part because it's the cheapest thing on the menu but also because you have a thing about eating in front of people, men, you don't know; going back to teenage years spent with braces, the horror of food caught in them. Risotto you can eat in tiny bites, and you don't even have to chew it. He orders the steak, *medium rare, of course*, and asks you if he should go for chunky chips or fries.

Go for chunky chips, the waitress says, the chunky chips

23

here are out of this world, and once she's said that, of course you have to say, Chunky chips.

When he says, What are we drinking, you gesture at your tap water: Just this is fine. But he insists on a glass of wine, then, Feck it, let's get a bottle, shall we? Oh, you say, but the *shall we* doesn't seem to be a question. He orders a bottle of white wine and you do the calculations in your head. There's no way you can afford this, what with him ordering the steak too. Just risotto and tap water and a euro for the tip, you can manage. If you have half a glass of wine and just pay for that, say adding five euro, instead of paying for half of the twenty-five-euro bottle? But he's already filled your glass right up and is raising his, Your good health, sláinte, and you find yourself taking a gulp. Slow down. You can put it on your mum's credit card, which you still have for emergencies, and when she asks you can say there was a problem with yours, or something, you'll think of something.

You try to focus on the conversation. You're aware you haven't contributed much: this can't be fun for him, forced to do all the talking. You try to think of interesting questions to ask or witty things to say but your mind is a blank. You don't know if you're allowed to ask what he's working on now. You think of your mum that time, going to see a prize-winning author in town. Your mum had loved her book, had bought a copy for you, and several friends. When the Q&A began, your mum asked the author if she'd consider a sequel. From her velvet chair on the stage, the author heaved an exaggerated sigh and rolled her eyes. If I had a dollar, she said, for every time I was asked that, I wouldn't need to be here, any other questions?

The food comes, and he hasn't yet mentioned your stories. He will, you tell yourself, he will.

You eat your risotto, and when he insists that you try his you don't say you're vegetarian, but just take a polite single chip and try to ignore the sauce.

The wine goes down much faster than it should. He orders a glass of red as well. His cheeks are pink.

You finish your risotto and lay your cutlery neatly down. Any moment now, you think.

He pushes his plate aside.

I'm away to the jacks, he says.

While he's gone, the waitress comes to clear the plates. Are yez finished?

That was lovely, thanks, you say as she lifts yours.

Did yez like the chunky chips, she says. She lowers her voice conspiratorially: They fry them three times, that's the secret. Then she goes on: Will your da be wanting a doggy bag, she says, for the remains of his steak. Oh, you fumble, feeling your cheeks get hot, I don't think so, thank you anyway.

What's that? he says then, coming back to the table, zipping his flies.

Oh, nothing, you say quickly, she just said would you be wanting a doggy bag.

And what did you say? he says, looking amused.

I said, you say, still flustered, I didn't know.

Sure why would I be wanting a doggy bag?

Maybe you have a dog, you say, stupidly, and he puts his elbow dramatically on the table and leans his head on his fist and says, *Oh really?* Do I *look* like the sort of person who has a dog?

I don't know, you say, and he says, Tell me this, so if I'd a dog, what sort of dog would it be?

And all you can think is St Bernard, the flecks of spittle on fleshy pink lips, now suddenly so close, but of course you can't say that, and so you just haver, say nothing, smile, smile, smile, and he puts a paw over yours, the black hairs on the backs of his white fingers, and he says, Now you'd be a whippet, wouldn't you, or what do you call them ones with all the hair, a saluki, that's it, that's what you'd be. All jumpy and nervy and skittish. Relax, just relax!

And the horror of it all somehow galvanises you and you manage to blurt out: My stories. Can we talk about my stories?

Your stories? he says, as if you've said something funny. Then he sits back, freeing your hand from his. Ok. Fair enough. Your stories. Well, he says. What do you think about your stories?

Me? you say. I don't know what I think. I mean I wondered what you think.

Well, do you think they're any good?

I don't know, you say. Well, no, not really. I mean I know they're only drafts, but – I'm just not sure what to do with them next, or—

Or what?

Or if they might be good enough to, I don't know, to send somewhere. Or something.

Look, he says, I'll be honest with you. Your stories are. What would the word be. Your stories are *facile*. They're just too facile. There's nothing there – is there?

I – don't know, you say.

Well then, there you go, he says. If you *knew*, you'd know.

Ok, you say.

For the first time all meal, there is a silence. It is horrible. You can feel him watching you, watching as you try not to cry, watching as you try and fail not to cry.

When the waitress comes back with the dessert menu she looks at you, looks from you to him.

Just the bill, he says.

He lets you split it, seems happy to, in fact. You are shaking now, and can't seem to stop the tears from spilling endlessly down your face. Your mum has paid for this, you keep on thinking. You feel so stupid, so wretchedly stupid. Oh, come on now, he finally says. You wouldn't want me to tell you like it isn't, would you? Don't take it so personally.

When you finally get out of the restaurant, he suggests a drink back at the hotel bar. You manage to say no: you couldn't bear for anyone, anyone else, to see you like this, but he says he's walking back that way anyway, so what else can you do? You walk back together.

The hotel lobby is full of people, writers, workshop attendees, festival organisers, all streaming out of the closing-night session and into the bar. No one sees you, or everyone does, you can't tell.

Look, you're taking this too personally, he says again, and he offers to see you to your room.

Please, you say, meaning *no, please no, please no*, and you manage to turn and make it to the stairs and he doesn't, he doesn't follow.

In your washbag you have a little blister-strip of Valium, the generic sort, brought back by your flatmate's boyfriend from his trip to India. The dosage depends on whether or not you're used to it: you're not. Would two tablets be enough? you think.

Enough for what?

Enough to just fall asleep, enough never to have to deal with any of this again, this suffocating *shame*.

Don't be such a fucking idiot.

What, after all, has happened? Nothing. You try to imagine telling it as a story – writing it. You went for dinner with someone who didn't think your writing was much good.

And, what?

He momentarily touched your *hand*?

Nothing. Nothing has happened.

You can hear the revelry downstairs. It's only, you think, just beginning. The nights here are legendary: the bar stays open until the last people have gone, which is sometimes when the first are coming down for breakfast. The writer will be there, the people from the workshop, the other writers, the other people from the other workshops. All of the organisers, the audience members, the volunteers. You could call your mum but of course you can't call your mum. Breathe, you think, just breathe. The air in your room smells stale, though there are signs everywhere saying *No Smoking!* It's in the fabric of the curtains, you think, and the carpet and the polyester quilt and the matching pelmet around the bed, and *pelmet*, what a ridiculous word. You open the window the two inches that it opens and the cool green air rushes in. If your laptop weren't so expensive you'd hurl it out of the window and into the river somewhere below. No you wouldn't, of course you wouldn't. Somewhere below, on the river path, people are laughing.

Did I tell you this story is true?

Something's Coming

'A CLOUD IS COMING,' our younger son was chanting in a toneless monologue. 'Some wind is coming. Another cloud is coming.'

We'd given up asking him to be quiet. My husband, teeth gritted, was trying to keep the car as steady as possible over the bumps and potholes: we'd already had to stop, twice, for each child to be sick into the blackberry bushes and tangled thorny shrubs encroaching on the lane. Our elder son was hunched over the Tamagotchi my husband had bought him from some overpriced shop in Shoreditch, which wasn't helping with the carsickness, but it would die, Finn kept tearfully insisting, or at the very least morph into some kind of monster, if he neglected it now.

'We used to do that on purpose,' my husband said, 'just to see what would happen', and Finn blinked at him behind his new red glasses, pale and serious.

The Tamagotchi beeped.

'It's crying again,' Finn said. 'I don't know what it wants. What does it *want*?'

'Is it hungry,' I said, 'or have you maybe overfed it? Or maybe it wants to sleep, or play?'

'I've tried all of those things,' Finn said. 'I've tried *all* of them.'

'Then I can't help you, pet, but I'm sure it will be fine.'

'And now some rain – some rain is coming,' Joseph droned. 'And something else. Something-else is coming.'

'Still nothing?' my husband said.

'Nope,' I said, holding up my phone uselessly to the ceiling. 'Wait, one bar. No – gone. It's fine,' I said. 'We'll come out somewhere. We have to come out somewhere.'

The Tamagotchi chirruped.

'It's evolving,' Finn cried. 'The screen's gone black. Now it's clearing again. It's bigger and – look, it's got horns. Are horns good or bad? Daddy! Are horns good or bad?'

'Dan,' I said, and my husband said, 'Oh, good, definitely good.'

'But, Daddy, are you *sure*?'

'The something-else is coming, *the something-else is coming.*'

'Joseph, pet, Finn, could you both pipe down for a minute?'

'But what if horns are *bad*?'

'The something-else is bad. It's going to be here any minute now.'

'Finn!' I said. '*Jo*seph. Please!'

'Here it comes. The something-else.'

On cue the sky darkened and there was a sudden squall of rain.

'Joseph,' I said. 'It's rain. It's only rain.'

'Where does he get it from?' my husband said.

'I think horns are bad, Daddy. I really think that horns are bad.'

'Where do they *both* get it from, Jesus, Finn, just press buttons A and C and kill it and start again.'

'Daddy! I *can't* do that, I can't just *kill* it!'

'Daniel—'

'Daddy said *Jesus*. That's a bad, bad word.'

'It's not a *bad* word, Joseph, it's just a word you shouldn't say, and Daddy's sorry, aren't you, Daddy – Dan.'

'I'm certainly sorry we're not on a beach somewhere sunny right now.'

'Oh, for crying out loud.'

'Crying won't help, nothing will help, now the bad thing's here.'

'Right,' I snapped, 'I've had enough of this, both of you. Joseph, quiet. Finn, give me that thing right now.'

I reached behind and took the keyring from him.

'Don't kill it, Mummy. Please don't kill it.'

'I'm not going to kill it, I'm not going to kill anything.' The little horned creature was leaping about on the screen. It did look kind of evil. Stop it, I told myself. I held down buttons A and B. 'There. That's it paused. Let's all just – take a breath and work out where we are.'

'Are we lost?'

'No, Finn, we're not *lost*.'

'But you just said you don't know where we are.'

'Well, we're here, aren't we? We're here on this road. And all roads have to end somewhere.'

'There's more,' droned Joseph, calmly. 'There's more of the something-else. It's begun now.'

My husband thumped the steering wheel. 'Jesus Christ!'

'*Dan.*'

We crawled on in silence.

Whose idea had it been to spend our precious fortnight of holiday driving round country lanes in the rain in the back arse of nowhere, with children who got carsick?

I'd only myself to blame.

We'd left it, of course, until the very last minute. Dan had wanted Thailand, or the Caribbean, somewhere far-flung and luxurious. He'd insisted he'd a couple of big shoots lined up for the autumn, but I'd seen these things fall through before and so I'd put my foot down – the long-haul flight, the jet lag, the exorbitance of it all. We could have gone to the Algarve, where my dad lived now. But I wanted the boys to have the kind of summer holidays I used to have, or at least the sort I remembered having. Van Morrison playing in the car, or my parents' battered old Chieftains tape. Blackberry-picking and deserted white-sand beaches, Aran jumpers and sandwiches eaten in the opened boot of the car. I wanted them to feel, at least a tiny bit, Irish. Sometimes I thought I couldn't bear that they were growing up with posh little London accents, wore mini-versions of their dad's own limited-edition trainers, considered London Fields *the countryside*.

All of this amused Dan no end. He pointed out that if the boys weren't Irish, they weren't Jewish either – he'd left all that behind, and didn't mind. But we still went to Friday-night suppers at his mum's, and the boys liked lighting the candles on the menorah, getting chocolate money at Hanukkah. Now that I'd left Belfast – now that even my dad had left Belfast – we had nothing there, no roots, no connection, unless I made the effort to forge it.

So here we were, offbeat, off-grid, and very nearly off the map in Donegal, staying in an eco-cottage two minutes from the wild Atlantic Ocean, once some kind of fisherman's bothy, haphazardly extended, the nearest neighbours two miles up the track. Wood-burning stoves, a composting toilet, water heated (at least in theory) by the solar panels on the roof – and no mains electricity, so *here* we were making the daily hour-long (or two, or this time likely three) round trip to somewhere, anywhere, we could charge our phones and iPads and Kindle Fires and battery packs, and deal with all the emails that couldn't be fobbed off with autoreplies.

And despite what I'd said to Finn, I was beginning to fear that we really were lost.

One lane looked exactly like another: that was the problem. They wound round, doubled back on themselves, came to sudden and inexplicable ends, petering out to dirt tracks where you weren't sure if they'd widen into roads again, or at least an impression of them, or end entirely. Our hire car was already scratched on both sides and the clutch was beginning to give off a funny scorched smell. Dan, being Dan, had blithely ignored the *fully comprehensive* insurance hard-sold to us by the boy behind the rental counter.

And the rain was getting heavier.

I'd forgotten how capricious the weather was here: the way you could watch storms brewing, twisting, racing in from the Atlantic, suddenly upon you. Out of nowhere the skies would darken and the rain lash down, then with no warning it would stop, and a brilliant glittering sunlight break through. At times it was almost exhilarating.

Now, though, even on full pelt, the wipers were battering back and forth ineffectually. Dan turned on the sidelights, and then the headlights proper. The car splashed and jounced and jolted. The boys, save the occasional moan, were silent. Joseph looked to be muttering something under his breath – at least, his lips were moving, but no sound was coming out. Finn was blinking too much.

'Isn't this an adventure,' I said brightly. I raised my voice above the noise of the car and the wind and the rain to say it, and the voice that came out wasn't mine: it was my mum's. For a vertiginous second she was me and I was a child again and it was impossible that I'd grown up, married, somehow had kids of my own – impossible that I ever would do so. The car seemed to stop moving. Everything seemed to stop as if none of it, this, was real.

I dug my nails into my fists and exhaled the way the therapist had taught me until I felt myself recolonising my body.

Six years now. Seven years next April. Mum had never

got to meet either of my boys, her only grandchildren, though she'd known that I was pregnant with Finn; had helped me choose his name, or at least indulged the pretence of it. I'd been eight or nine weeks pregnant at the time, far too early to know if the baby was a boy or a girl. Mum had thought girl, or so she'd said, but by the time we'd found out, she was gone. Most days, these days, I was mostly fine, but then out of nowhere I'd suddenly miss her with every single atom of my body and soul.

'Mummy,' said Finn. 'Mummy, I'm going to be sick again. I'm going to be sick again, Mummy.'

Mum, I said in my head. *Mum, if you're there, please help me.* But there was only me.

'Hang on, sweetheart,' I said, scrabbling to pass Finn a plastic bag. 'Dan, stop the car. Stay there, Finn, I'm coming round to help you.'

Finally, the lane widened into something resembling a road, and then an indisputable road, and then – the relief! – we were coming into a town, or what passed for a town in these parts. A wool shop, windows strung with Molloy blankets, next to a shop selling bolts of tweed. A pub, a Centra, a small hotel. The rain was still coming down, but no longer more than the wipers could cope with. We found the town's car park, next to a forlorn and dismal-looking playground, and made a dash for the hotel; burgers and chips for the boys, leek-and-potato soup and thick dark wheaten bread for me, and for all of our starved devices, glorious, limitless electricity.

Curled up in an armchair by the open fire, I watched my boys. Finn and Joseph uplit by the blue of their screen, sharing, for once, almost nicely. Joseph's little green-and-yellow glasses, the little yellow stay-puts coiled round his sticking-out ears. They'd barely picked at their burgers. But then again, they had spent all morning being carsick. Dan, on the other hand, was eating microwaved apple pie and ice cream like a proverbial little boy. Oh Dan, in his immaculate uncreased Barbour and peach-and-grey trainers already destined not to survive the trip, his ironic Fair Isle jumper, or whatever the Icelandic version was called, from the stag weekend in Reykjavik – I felt a rush of love for him, for all of them. We were going to survive this, came the thought unprompted into my head: again, a voice not mine. We were – *what?*

'What is it?' said Dan, looking up, and I shook my head and forced a smile.

'Nothing,' I said.

We went into the Centra to buy fresh supplies – there was no fridge in the eco-cottage, only an outside larder, and the suggestion that you kept milk and perishables in the stream to cool them. The boys, petulant and grumbling now, wanted a Magnum, and I said no: we were about to get into the car. There was a box of toys by the tills, teddy bears and cuddly rabbits and wooden trains, with a handwritten sign saying they were free to good homes, and they started rummaging through to see if there was anything they might like, becoming deliberately aggressive, shoving each other and squabbling. I shouted at them and immediately felt terrible. Our little city boys: of course they hadn't wanted to leave the warm hotel, their iPad, of course they didn't want to go back to the cold, dank cottage, were bored of collecting stones on the shore, didn't care that these little striped pebbles of metamorphic gneiss, according to the visitors' book, dated back to around 1.7 billion years ago, didn't like the muddy scramble up the cliff to look again at some boring, bleak old view.

Next time, I thought, maybe I'd just let Dan have his way and get a villa somewhere sunny with maid service and a pool. I'd try not to worry about affording it, about notions of Irishness, and all of us would be happier.

'Look,' I found myself saying, 'why don't you have a Magnum, we are on holiday. I'll go get the car and pull up right outside, there's no need for all of us to get soaked again.'

The boys stared at me. It was Dan who let them have ice creams half an hour before their dinner, or Haribo, or bought them magazines they'd never look at for the plastic tat that came free. I was always the one saying no.

'Well, quickly,' I said, 'before I change my mind', and they rushed off down the aisle to the freezer chest.

'You're a star,' said Dan, already digging the car keys from his pocket. 'I might as well send a couple more emails while there's signal.'

'Go for it,' I said. 'I'll see you out the front in ten.'

So I fetched the car, Dan loaded the boot and the boys got in, and we set off. Narrow, unfamiliar roads in relentless rain: it takes more concentration than you'd think. We'd been driving for half an hour or more when I realised that the boys were too quiet: no fighting, no wriggling, no chanting or silly songs.

'Do you feel sick?' I said. They each had a fresh plastic bag on their laps; I'd insisted. 'Dan,' I said, and he looked up from his phone, which just about still had internet. 'If I'm driving, you've got to be more on it.' I hated my tone of voice even as I said it – so bossy, school-marmy. I felt him rolling his eyes. Annoyed, I craned my neck to see the back seat properly – the mirrors were still adjusted for Dan, who'd been doing most of the driving.

I almost crashed.

'What's *that* doing there?' I said. 'Dan?'

'What's what doing where?' he said, still sounding pissed off.

'That,' I said. 'That – thing.' Sitting in between the boys was a china doll, skirt neatly spread, little brown lace-up boots. She had a round white face with painted rosy cheeks, a rosebud mouth, and her eyes, a bright, bright blue, seemed to be taking everything in.

'She wants to be part of our family,' said Joseph.

'The man said we should have her,' said Finn.

'What have I told you about taking things from strangers?' I said.

'But we didn't take her, Mummy,' Finn said, on the verge of tears. 'The man just said we should have her.'

39

'What man?' I said. 'Daniel, what's this all about?'

'I have no idea,' he said, 'I was on my phone. Chill out, it's just a doll. Why shouldn't the boys have a doll if they want?'

'She wants to be ours,' said Joseph again.

'That box was meant for children who don't have any toys,' I said.

'Actually, it just said "free to a good home",' said Dan sharply. 'Is that not what we are? Are we not a good home?'

There wasn't an answer I could give to that, so I just kept driving.

Later that night. The boys – finally – asleep in their bunks in the odd little room down the flagstone corridor; Dan and I sprawled in the thick sheepskins on the settle, drinking red wine. In August, in Donegal, the sun doesn't set until half nine, ten, and the last of the light still lingers for a good hour more. The visitors' book said there were often seals in the bay that came chasing shoals of mackerel and pollock, and we'd been watching for them. We'd been talking idly, in that casual, intimate way I'd almost forgotten, given the chaotic daily scramble of bedtime and tantrums and one or the other of us needing to be out, and, if we weren't, of coordinating diaries then slumping in front of something on Netflix.

I didn't have the words to say it to Dan, but I'd started to feel we didn't know each other any more. We exchanged necessary information about our days, the boys, to-do lists, but we never *talked*. That had been an ulterior motive for this holiday too, part of the appeal of the eco-cottage and its proud lack of signal or wi-fi: to disconnect from everything so that the two of us could reconnect, or try to.

I'd been telling him about the manuscript I was reading, by an Irish author I'd poached from a rival publishing house: the first in a young adult trilogy about the Crone, the Bone Mother, in Irish the Cailleach, who took what needed to die to make way for the new coming in.

The otherworld, in Irish cosmology, was not an after-life, but rather a parallel world to our own which could, given the right conditions, be entered and left. Some could do this at will, and some stumbled into it by chance. The book was about four siblings, two girls and two boys, who found they had the ability to cross worlds, one long summer when their mother was sick and they were bundled off to rural relatives. The trilogy was named after an ancient Irish poem, according to which there were three great Ages: the age of the yew tree, the age of the eagle, the age of the Cailleach. *The Age of the Yew Tree* ended with the youngest sister simply deciding not to come back. But there were fundamental problems with the plot that the author had yet to solve, and I'd put aside other, more pressing manuscripts in order to bring it to Donegal with me. Otherworlds – ageless Irish witches – curses – lost children: I'd had a feeling it would make more sense here, and it did. The wind whistling down the stovepipe and around the cottage's corners, the restlessly rattling pebbles on the beach. Was it Brendan Behan who had said, *I am a daylight atheist?*

I shivered. Dan reached round me to tuck the blanket in.

'I'm fine,' I said. 'Thank you.'

I got up.

'Where are you going?' he said.

'Just to check on the boys.'

It was dark in the corridor that led to their bedroom. I'd to turn on the torch on my phone. The flagstones were cold underfoot, even through two pairs of socks. The old oak door of their bedroom didn't want to let me in: it jammed on the floor, where the wood had swollen; groaned. I forced it, slipped in, stooped to check on Joseph in the lower bunk, then stood on my tiptoes to see Finn in the upper. Both boys looked pale and soft and undefended, even under the weight of the blankets and quilts we'd heaped on them. It was meant to be peaceful, watching a sleeping child, but it had always just given me the shivers, how helpless they were.

Finn's Tamagotchi chirruped and I jumped. It was on the pillow beside him and had somehow come unpaused: the creature was capering about the screen, horns longer now. It had buds on its back too, where the tips of leathery wings seemed to be coming through. I went to pause it again, then found myself pressing and holding buttons A and C instead. The little creature jumped and jumped at me. Die, I thought. Come on, hurry up, *die*. It keeled over sideways and the screen went black. A mound with a cross appeared, and for a few seconds some kind of weird ghost hovered. Then the screen blacked out again and when it cleared a new egg had appeared. There. I laid it back on Finn's pillow.

Finn squirmed in the glare of my phone torch. I pointed it away, quickly, and it fell on the doll, sitting primly on the dresser beside the two little pairs of folded-up glasses. It was only the torchlight, of course, that quivered across the china face and pursed lips, that made the eyes glint. But I picked her – *it* – up and took it with me back into the living room, where I zipped it into Dan's ridiculous Belstaff weekender that bristled with too many buckles and straps. I did up all of them. We would take it back to the Centra tomorrow.

Dan had got up too, while I'd been gone, to light the oil lamp and the candles.

'Close the curtains,' I said.

'There's no one watching. There's nobody for miles.'

'Just – close them anyway.'

He shrugged and did it. Without the restless, endless sea, the room suddenly felt shut in. If I raised my arms, I could place both hands flat on the ceiling.

'Actually, open them again,' I said.

Dan stood there, grinning in the flickering light.

'What?' I said.

'I'm not saying anything.'

'Well, don't.'

'But you have to admit that you are always a little bit crazy—'

'Seriously.'

43

'A day or two before—'

'Don't say it.'

'Ok, fine.'

He didn't.

We opened the curtains again; poured more wine; got back onto the settle. It occurred to me that my period had already been due for a day or two now: you sort of lost track of the days a bit here. Or at least I thought it had; it had been irregular recently. When I'd gone to the doctor about it, she'd said, Well, you're forty now, that's what starts to happen. There were blood tests you could have, to get an accurate picture of your fertility age, but I'd said no: I didn't want to know. Dan and I had always joked about our age gap – not that it was really a gap, three years – but lately I'd started to feel it. He could just go on and on – I couldn't.

Dan half-wanted a third. I three-quarters didn't, even if this was my last chance to. Go figure, I thought to myself, the maths of that one.

I couldn't help thinking, with a touch of bitterness, that it was simpler for him. I mean of course it was: if we did have another, he didn't have to do the *having*. But on a more abstract level, everything was simpler. He was an irrepressibly can-do person, which is what I both loved and couldn't stand about him. Nothing was a problem. A third baby? Fine, we'd hire a nanny. Flat too small? No worries, he'd land a couple of jobs and we'd rent somewhere bigger. If I did turn out to be pregnant, he'd be pleased. I felt a sudden flash of almost hatred for him.

'We're taking that doll back first thing tomorrow,' I said.

'Fine,' he said. 'I mean, if that's how you want to spend our time.'

'What else are we going to do, anyway?'

'Well, it's you who wanted this.'

'And I've already said, we won't do it again. Happy?'

'Oh, yes, I'm happy,' he said. 'This is a super holiday, best ever.'

For a long moment, neither of us spoke.

Why don't we call it quits and go back early? I wanted to say. But it felt like it would be more than the holiday we'd be giving up on.

I took a breath. 'Sorry,' I said. 'I am on edge. I feel guilty. I feel – responsible.'

'Look,' he said, and sighed as well. 'It's fine. We'll go away somewhere nice for half term – ok?'

'Ok,' I said, and leaned my head on his shoulder. 'Did I ever tell you?' I said after a bit. 'I had this homestay with a woman who was obsessed with dolls. She had dozens of them. Everywhere. The favourites used to get bibs tied on and put in high chairs. We had to sit there while she pretended to spoon-feed these things their Cheerios.'

'You've never told me that,' he said, in the half-playful, half-accusatory tone of someone who knows all your stories, or thinks they do. 'Are you sure you didn't get that from one of your authors?'

'Seriously,' I said. 'I swear. It was this cross-community thing, the summer I turned fifteen. They flew you to America and you stayed with American families for a fortnight. And the woman we were with – I haven't thought of this in years – she bathed her dolls, put them to bed at night. Read them stories, sang them songs. She was convinced they all had personalities.'

Dan's eyebrows were still raised.

'Cross my heart and hope to die,' I added dramatically, as fifteen-year-old me might have done, making the sign over my chest.

He shook his head and laughed. 'You've totally got that from somewhere.'

We sat for a bit. It did seem implausible. The room I remembered was a room you might once have dreamed: rows of shelves with dolls and dolls arranged, some china-limbed and others with artfully flushed cheeks and eyelashes, real cascading hair. All those vacant, cunning pairs of eyes.

'Princess Diana died,' I said. 'While we were staying there. The woman woke us in the middle of the night to say. We were both on the sofa-bed in the living room, because neither of us wanted the room with the dolls' cribs. And she came in, told us to get up right away – we didn't know what on earth was happening. And then Fionnuala – that was the other girl's name – Fionnuala said' – I started to laugh – '"Sure why would we care about some auld English princess", and your woman just *stared* at us, her face, I actually thought she might slap us? She considered herself proudly Irish American, that's why she was doing the whole thing in the first place, but she was utterly bewildered, like *we* were the freaky ones, and we couldn't help it, we just started pissing ourselves laughing. Oh God,'

I said, 'and the whole time she was cradling one of her little ones – that's what she called them – and she got cross with us then and said she'd never get it back to sleep.'

The woman's face swam up at me for a moment, her goggling eyes. When she'd left us that night, had we laughed at her too loudly? Had we done impressions of her, and had Fionnuala mocked the 'little ones' until, though still laughing myself, I begged her to stop, because however weird the woman was, she was our host, and besides, I was scared that she might – what? That she might *curse* us? *Had* she cursed us? Had she come downstairs to ask us to be quiet, and had she said, *You are bad, bad girls, and this will come back one day to bite you in the ass*, and had we been shocked into silence then by the ugliness of the words, not so bad in and of themselves, but somehow obscene coming from her?

I wondered if Fionnuala remembered. I'd forgotten her surname but maybe I could find her somehow, Facebook or something. I reached automatically for my phone before remembering it was useless here.

'Croix de bois, croix de fer, si je mens je vais en enfer,' Dan said suddenly.

'You what?'

'Wooden cross, iron cross, if I lie I'll go to hell. We had this French au pair who used to say that all the time.'

'Stick a needle in my eye,' I said.

'Mandy,' he said. 'Is that right? Would you get a French au pair called Mandy? Or maybe that was another one. We had so many.'

'The woman had a daughter who'd run away,' I said, 'and they never found out what happened to her. She got her first doll just after, because it reminded her of her daughter as a baby.'

'Weird,' Dan said.

'Don't you think it's kind of sad?'

He laughed. 'I think it's really fucking creepy. Come on. Let's go to bed.'

But I couldn't sleep. Too much red wine, I thought: I wasn't used to drinking it, shouldn't be drinking at all, in fact, if there was even the slightest chance I could be pregnant. Things kept tumbling through my head. That silly little pixelated Tamagotchi as I'd killed it. Joseph saying, *Now the bad thing's here*, and, *It's begun*.

I needed a glass of water.

I sat up. Dan was gently snoring and didn't stir. What I could see of his slack, sleeping face looked entirely unfamiliar. I eased out of the covers. Our bedroom was just off the main living space, which was lit, now, by streaming moonlight. I padded through to the sink, drank straight from the tap. The water was brown and it tasted of ancient things. The boys, at first, had been disgusted, refused to drink it, refused to believe that water coming straight from a peat bog was less repulsive than London water which had been through a dozen people already.

I decided to check on the boys one last time. I hadn't

brought my phone with me; had to make my way along the corridor with my fingertips on the walls. There was a scuttling noise behind me. Mice, probably: a rural cottage like this was probably overrun with them. My heart was yammering in my chest. *I am a daylight atheist.*

And then I realised.

Dan's weekender bag. It had been unbuckled, unzipped. The last person to touch it, I was positive, had been me, when I shut the doll in. There would have been no reason for Dan to open it, because we just had our cables and chargers in there—

The doll had got out.

At the same moment I realised this I realised she – *it* – was behind me in the corridor.

Every single atom in my body froze.

I can't say how I knew, but I *knew*. I didn't know if it was me she wanted, or my boys, but I did know, without a doubt, that if I turned around that thing would launch itself at me, clutch at me with its brittle, gleeful fingertips.

Think. I tried to think. My mind raced through all the Irish myths I knew, half-knew, but there was nothing of any use. The corridor felt longer at night than in the day, but if I made a dash for it, could I get to the bedroom, slam the door?

I took a tiny, experimental step. And straight away there it was again: that juddery, sly, scuttery noise behind me – right behind me now.

Don't look, I told myself, don't look – and it took

49

everything I had, every fibre of my being, to stay stock-still and not to look, not submit to it, to this thing that wanted me, was just waiting for me to do so.

I wouldn't make the door to the bedroom in time, I knew that now.

I closed my eyes.

I couldn't summon up my mum, or for the life of me even a single line of a prayer, not the framed St Patrick's Breastplate hanging on the bedroom wall, or the Lord's Prayer drilled into us at primary school.

I couldn't scream either, for Dan, for help, even if I'd been able to, because the thing would feed on the slightest sound.

It was getting stronger already, I could feel it, the current of my despair flowing into it. I tried to pull my energy back, tried to visualise wrestling it into one of the wicker picnic baskets by the back door, filling the rest of the basket with those billion-year-old stones, strapping it shut, hurling it into the sea.

But it would bob free, wash back in on the tide, haul itself up the shore on chipped china fingers, skittering up to the house like a crab.

I could feel the doll smiling at the thought – insolent, beatific, triumphant. Whatever it was, curse or desire, whatever it wanted from me, it was winning. If you don't face your fears, I thought, they chase you for ever, feeding on you, swelling in strength till they consume you. You meet your destiny on the road you took to avoid it. How long had I known that something was coming?

Something's Coming

There was nothing for it but to open my eyes, and turn, slowly, all the way round in the cold, indifferent corridor, and face it.

Dark Matters

HIS SISTER LIFTS HIM FROM THE AIRPORT. He said he'd get a taxi, or the airport bus, but she was having none of it. She pulls in to the pick-up area and he doesn't notice her at first, not till she winds down the window and actually shouts at him. She has a new car since he's seen her last – a Ford Mondeo, mid-blue.

'Don't,' she says.

'Don't what?'

'Don't you be making any jokes about Mondeo Man.'

'I didn't say anything.'

'Tony got us a good trade-in deal. It was second-hand, but it's not a bad car. Bit big, maybe. Bigger than *you* need, anyways,' she says, looking pointedly at his backpack, which is all's the luggage he's brought. 'You not planning on staying? Problems of the universe to solve? Sorry,' she says, almost immediately, 'that was out of order', and exhausting as it is, it's a strange comfort, that this is still the Tanya he knows.

He slings his bag into the boot. Looks up at the low, damp sky. He always forgets how much it presses in on you. How rare it is here to have a high-skied day. He has no idea how long he'll be here for. When he got Tanya's message, he just came. Went online, booked the first flights he could, didn't even look at the cost, just put them on his credit card. Emailed the administrator of his programme from Geneva Airport, saying he'd be in touch when he knew more. It was interesting to see how easy it was to jettison everything.

He takes a breath, gets into the front seat.

'So how is she?' he says.

'If it wasn't for lockdown,' Tanya says, 'we might have gotten her to the GP earlier. But then again,' she says resolutely, 'we might not've, because you know Mum.'

Tanya puts her left arm behind the headrest of his seat as she cranes to reverse and pull a U-turn to get them out – a gesture, a posture, that's so much their dad that he smiles.

'What?' she says.

'Nothing.'

'No, seriously – what? It had better not be another fucking Mondeo joke.'

'I haven't made a first one yet. And it wasn't. Just you looked so like Dad there.'

'Wise up.'

'You really did.'

'Fuck off. You know I used to cry myself to sleep every night, the way you and Kevin would say I had his nose?'

'I mean, I've got to say . . .'

'You fucking dare,' she says, but she's laughing now. 'Yous were wee gobshites,' she says. 'I never looked anything like Dad, I was always the pure spit of Mum.' She stops. 'Well,' she says. 'The crazy thing is Mum doesn't even look bad? She just looks sort of – I don't know. Like she's had the puff knocked from her. Which, you know, is fair enough. It'd put a decade on anyone.'

He thinks that Tanya looks old. Her highlights need doing – she's half an inch of grey roots. And her skin is a web of lines around her eyes, the creases across her forehead, around her mouth, far deeper than he remembers – than they should be.

Tanya, he wants to say. When did you get old?

Instead he says, 'Me and Kev were wee bastards, right enough.'

'Aye,' she says. 'Yous were.' Then, as if to stop him saying anything more, she says, 'Now shut you up a minute while I get us in the right lane, I hate driving in rush hour.'

Finley opens the door to them, holding it with his shoulder, not looking up, intent on something on his phone.

'Hey, Finley,' he says to his shambling nephew who's now a match for him in height. 'Has your mum been putting you to sleep in a growbag?'

'Ha ha,' says Finley, shuffling backwards, still not looking up.

'For crying out loud,' says Tanya, 'would you ever get off that flipping thing.'

'Cool your jets, Ma,' says Finley, flat-packing himself up on the stairs, all knees and elbows.

He thinks: How did we all ever fit in here?

'Mummy?' Tanya's calling. 'Mummy, your prodigal son's returned. Finley, where's Granny?'

'I dunno,' he says.

'No, sure how would you. If I wanted a response from you I'd do better doing a wee dance and putting it on TikTok. Mummy? Where are you at, is everything ok?'

'Here, I'm here,' his mum says, from the top of the stairs. 'Och, wee son. And here you are.'

'Hi Mum,' he says.

Tanya said she didn't look bad, but she does, he thinks: she looks terrible. She walks down slowly, clutching at the banister, hunched over, like a wee auld lady with a hump. She stops while Finley unfolds himself and gets out of the way, and he puts out his hands to help her down the last couple of steps. Her hands in his are bony and they shake.

'C'mere to me, love. Och, wee son. C'mere to me.'

She clutches at his back, reaches up to draw down his face. The whites of her eyes are yellow, glistening.

'Mum,' he says.

'Look at you,' she says. 'Just look at you. My wee boy. Here, you must have a wild thirst on you after all that travelling. Tanya, love, away and put on the kettle.'

'Anything else you want me to do – slaughter a calf?'

'Not at all, just put some of them shortbread biscuits on a plate, I got the sort he likes, you'll take a wee biscuit, won't you, son?'

'Sure let me do it,' he says, glad of the excuse to turn for the kitchen.

'He'll not know where anything is,' says Tanya, coming in after him.

He opens a cupboard at random. There is a tub of Smash, a tub of Complan, a packet of Hobnobs, the new tin of Walker's shortbread, which he can't remember having any opinion on, and nothing else. He lifts down the tin, opens the fridge: a carton of skimmed UHT milk, a packet of sliced ham, a sliced white loaf, a tub of margarine.

'Jesus,' he says. 'No wonder she's got stomach cancer.'

'She's up at Kevin's for her tea on Tuesday and Thursday and we have her for the day on Sunday,' says Tanya, slamming mugs on a tray, 'so you may wind your neck in.'

'Is everything ok in there?'

'All under control,' Tanya says. 'Don't you worry, Mummy.'

'Now isn't this lovely,' his mum says, beaming round at them as they sip their tea and eat their biscuits, 'isn't this just lovely' – as if, he thinks, it was a celebration they were gathered for. 'All's we need's Kevin,' she goes on, 'and he's calling round tomorrow, so he is, Joanna's on lates at the moment and one of the girls is just getting over a wee bug so it's topsy-turvy for them. Here, you must go out for a drink while you're back,' she says, 'sure how often are the three of yous together. Up the Four Winds or something, do the pub quiz, wouldn't that be nice, I'm sure no one else would stand a chance. Och, wee son,' she says, beaming and leaning forward to squeeze his knee, 'it's just so good to have you back.'

'You should make the most of him,' Tanya says to Finley. 'He could help you with your science homework.'

'Sure I'm dropping it as soon as I can,' says Finley.

'Even so,' says Tanya. She turns to him. 'Why don't you tell our Fin something cool,' she says, 'like an experiment or something, see if you can fire him up.'

'Ok,' he says. 'Let me think.'

He lifts a *Take a Break* magazine and balances it on two tea mugs. 'Come here,' he says to Finley, 'stand here, so you're only looking at this from above. You're not allowed to move it, or in any way touch it – so if I put an object underneath, how can you tell what that object is?'

'Well, I can see it was your wallet,' Finley says.

'Pretend that you can't. What's the solution?'

'I dunno,' says Finley. 'X-ray vision?'

'Nope.'

'Em, going back in time?'

'Nope.'

'Is the answer that you're supposed to bend down and have a wee juke underneath?' says his mum. 'Change your perspective?'

'No, Mum. Ok, see, what you do is – if I'd some marbles, I could fire them underneath, and plot the angle and speed they bounced off whatever was hidden below. If I did that enough times, collected enough data, I'd have a fair idea of the shape and mass of the hidden object.'

'Oh right,' says Finley.

'That's basically particle physics in a nutshell,' he says.
'Well,' says his mum. 'Isn't that just fascinating.'

Tanya says she has to leave shortly, to take Finley to his
football practice. But first she brings him up to the back
bedroom, the room that used to be hers: it's stacked with
boxes all along one wall.

'We're to go through them all,' she says. 'Mum says she
doesn't want it to be a burden when she's gone, so I said
we'd do it now.'

He lifts the lid off a shoebox at random. It's packed with
comics – old *Beano*s and *Dandy*s.

'What did she want to be keeping these for?'

'She's kept everything – school reports, random jotters,
all of it. So you may make a start on it. How long are you
staying for, anyway?' Then Tanya answers herself, before he
has a chance to: 'I know, I know, "How long's a piece of
string." We'll talk it through with Kev and Joanna. Jo's
speaking to a colleague of hers works in palliative care.'

'And is that definitely—'

'It's what she says she wants. The chemo would only buy
her a couple of months and she says it's not worth the
suffering. Here, look,' she says, 'you don't know of any
experimental treatments that might help, do you?'

'I'm a particle physicist, Tanya.'

'I know, but – is there not maybe something they're
developing with, I don't know, tiny wee nano-particle

things, or radiation or something, that you could get her on a trial for?'

'I'm a particle physicist. I have no idea about cancer.'

'And you don't know anyone – like, anyone – who does?'

'Of course I don't.'

'And there's me thinking you were meant to be this Mr Big-Shot Famous Scientist Guy, so much better than the rest of us.'

'I don't know what I'm supposed to say,' he says. 'I'm here, aren't I? I came.'

Tanya glares at him. 'Aye,' she says. 'Hold on a minute while I find your fucking medal.'

Tanya's crying.

'Mummy's dying,' she says. 'In a couple of months she's going to be dead. Gone.'

'There's nothing I can do,' he says.

'And the irony is you're the one she dotes on. Her wee blue-eyed boy. Wanging on about playing marbles.'

'Tanya,' he says.

After they've gone, he cooks a frozen pepperoni pizza for himself, picking off the pepperoni, and makes his mum a mug of Complan. She insists on folding out the extra leaf on the dining room table for him, and fusses and footers about making sure he's got everything he wants. She chatters on too, in between spoonfuls of Complan, about what so-and-so's daughter named her grandchild, and about so-and-so that he was at school with, people, names, that are lost to him, if ever they were anything. Then she says, 'Talking of school. I rang them up, so I did, and said you'd go in and talk to them.'

'Why? About what?'

'Och, sure, what do you think! About physics! About CERN and that. Don't be looking at me like that. How often is it that someone from these parts works on a par with Einstein?'

'I don't work on a par with Einstein, Mum. I train computer programs to analyse and replicate mathematical datasets so we can see if there are anomalies that might be worthy of further analysis.'

'It's no point trying to explain it to me, sure my head's melted. Anyways, they're delighted to have you. Tomorrow, I said you'd be in, eleven o'clock.'

'What am I supposed to say?'

'How am I supposed to know,' she says with a laugh, as if he's made a joke. She gets to her feet and kisses him on the top of his head. 'All them brains in there,' she says. Then she says, 'I'm awful tired, son. Tell you the truth, I haven't been sleeping great. If it's ok with you, I might just take myself up for the night.'

'Of course, Mum,' he says. 'Here, leave all that, I'll see to it. Let me give you a hand up the stairs.'

He hovers outside her bedroom door while she shuffles out of her slippers then gets undressed and into bed.

'Okey-dokey then, Mum,' he says. 'Night-night.'

'Here, son,' she calls.

'Yes?'

'C'mon in,' she says, adding, 'I'm decent, if that's what you're worried about.'

He opens the door.

'Pull up a pew, why don't you, and sit with me a wee minute.'

'Alright,' he says. 'Sure.'

So he gets the chair from her dressing table, lifting the blouse and slacks, still warm and soft with her, and laying them instead across the end of the bed. He sets the chair next to her pillow, sits down. He clears his throat. His heart is suddenly beating fast.

'I'm sorry, Mum,' he says.

'Och, none of that, wee son. Just talk to me for a bit.'

'Ok,' he says.

'About anything.'

'Right.'

'Why don't you just tell me where they're at,' she says. 'With the science and that. The cutting edge of things. I don't even mind if I don't understand.'

She closes her eyes.

He racks his brains for something to tell her.

'They've managed to quantum-entangle tardigrades,' he says eventually.

'They've managed to what-what?'

'It's a quantum superstate, where two particles can't be described independently of the other.'

'I'll take your word for it.'

'They, so they basically got these tardigrades – water bears, you might know them as . . .'

'What, like you used to have in that wee plastic tank?'

'No, that was sea monkeys.'

'Aye. Where you'd to add the eggs to water, with that wee sachet of stuff, and watch for them to grow.' She chuckles. 'You were always so disappointed with them, so you were. Rushing in from school to see had they hatched and grown, but they were only ever wee shrimpy things that never did anything, and who was it had to flush them down the toilet, but muggins here.' She chuckles again. 'So what are they after doing to them now, then?'

'Not sea monkeys – water bears.'

'Och aye, you said.'

'They – well, they've done all sorts of things with them. Exposed them to high temperatures, frozen them, blasted them with UV – even cosmic rays. And they always manage to survive – they're pretty much like cockroaches, their resilience. And they wanted to know, these researchers, whether or not you could quantum-entangle a multi-cellular organism. That means, basically, they become bound to one another so that a change in one instantaneously affects the other.'

'Right,' she says.

'So tardigrades were the obvious candidate, and they collected three of them – I think from a roof gutter. Cooled them to a fraction of a degree above absolute zero, which is the lowest temperature that is theoretically possible – equivalent to minus 273.15 degrees C – and put them between the capacitator plates of a superconductor circuit, then coupled that to a second circuit. Then when they thawed them out – well, two died, but the other one could be said to be entangled. So they're claiming, anyway.'

'Entangled with what?'

'Well – the others. That shared the same qubit.'

'But you're just after saying they died.'

'Well, yes.'

'So what's the use in that, then?'

'To demonstrate that it's possible. I mean the implications of it – who knows, even death . . .'

There is a long and unexpectedly heavy silence. He has said something, he realises, that he shouldn't. Of course he has: why on earth is he talking about death to his mum, who is dying, literally, Stage 4, multiple secondaries, inoperable, two to four months?

'As I say,' he adds after a bit, 'it's not my field.'

For a while, there is silence. He looks round the room: the big mahogany wardrobe that they used to hide in, and pretend was Narnia, until she'd threaten to skelp them for creasing her good clothes. The matching dressing table, with its three-part mirror, the central oval and the two hinged rectangles, all slightly blotched, he can see that from here. The stripes on her bed's lilac pelmet that have been bleached by the sun. The cheapness of the sateen of her matching quilted counterpane. It's like a time warp, this room, or like a room that people have left one day and should never have come back to. The gravitational pull of home, he thinks, and the way it warps time . . .

She says, suddenly, 'I wonder can you still get them.'

'Get what, Mum?'

'Those wee sea monkey things. I wonder would Finley like them? Och, but sure they were always a wee bit disappointing, weren't they. I remember you rushing in from school to juke at them, to see had they done anything. But they never had, sure they hadn't. They never had.'

He sits there as her breathing lengthens, catches and lengthens. Her mouth is open and her face is slack. It feels too intimate, seeing her like this. Her thin hair unwashed against the faded floral pillowcase, like limp clusters of dandelion seeds. The orange-and-blue box of Fybogel sachets on her bedside table beside a tidemarked glass. He is too conscious now of the lavender-scented sachets she uses in her drawers, and below them a faintly urinous tang in the air. He wants to yank it all off, throw open the windows, air the place. Instead, he makes himself get slowly to his feet, draws the slippery counterpane up a little so it doesn't fall off if she turns, replaces her clothes over the back of the chair, and leaves.

The next day he goes back to his old school, as promised. The same as it always was: the curve of the driveway up from the gate, the same trees. He hesitates at the main

64

building, his feet wanting to continue round the driveway and across the quad, then goes up the steps to the main entrance, the heavy oak door that you only ever go through for an open day, or with your parents. The PA to the principal greets him – still the same woman, there for thirty-nine years, she tells him, and she tells him they're very proud of his achievements. She signs him in and takes him through those familiar corridors, past the G1 lecture theatre where you went for your sex education film, and to the hall, where the principal, a different principal, introduces him to an audience of all those taking physics, maths or further maths for A-level, and some of the brighter of the GCSE cohort.

He says the things he imagines the school wants them to hear: his own route from these very corridors to physics at Manchester University, then via postdoctoral research to the CMS experiment at CERN. He tells them some general things about physics: that it is an observational science, and we only know things to the precision with which we're able to measure them. That in particle physics you have an idea and you try to disprove it. From the fissling and the whispering, he can tell that their polite attention is flagging, that he's pitching it wrong, and so he deviates from his lecture notes and instead starts to talk about the discovery of the Higgs. They were looking, he says, trying to make it sound as if he is humbly referring to himself as part of a larger group, rather than co-opting his colleagues' work, for the one-in-a-trillion collisions you get with its distinctive energy signature. He uses the metaphor he once heard one of those colleagues use on TV: how it is like trying to detect an elephant at a watering hole, only all the animals have long departed, and you're going by a mess of footprints, and this is an elephant that can disguise itself as a rhino, or a gazelle, or maybe even one of those birds, you know, that flies into hippopotamuses' mouths to pick their teeth . . .

He can feel himself talking too fast, too wildly. He takes a sip of water and pretends to study his notes. There is nothing there to help him. He looks up and out at the faces.

'It was actually pure luck,' he says. 'Its mass turned out to be just right for the Large Hadron Collider to find it: a hundred and twenty-five gigaelectronvolts. I mean, it couldn't have been better, with regard to what's observable in terms of decay. And as soon as it was found, some people said, of course we found it, the LHC was built to find it. And yes, we knew we would definitely find it sooner or later – but only if it existed. And how on earth could we have known that in advance? We didn't – couldn't. Because we know nothing,' he says. 'Really – we know nothing. We have to comport ourselves as if we do, maybe we even have to believe that we do, but we don't. People talk about "looking at the face of the universe", but the universe doesn't have a face, that's just our projection. We have to unsee what we see, or think we see – all of it. I mean, look at us,' he says. 'What are we doing here? What are we doing? I'll tell you a secret,' he says. 'I'm here because of my mum.'

A couple of people laugh, uncertainly.

'No, seriously,' he says. 'I don't mean in a biological sense. I'm only here because my mum rang up and said I'd come in.'

A few more laughs.

The principal interjects brightly: He's sure they'd all love to know what it's *like* to work at CERN. 'So why don't you tell us,' the principal says, 'about your first time there.'

He takes a deep breath, out through the nose for a count of six, nods, has another sip of water. Thinks with an unexpected pang about that first time there. The monastic rooms at the hostel, the single bed and desk, the illusion that you could strip your life down to this, just this. Waking in the morning to the snow on the Alps, and opening the window to the purity of that air. The irrational sense that thinking itself would be easier here, faster, cleaner somehow, detached from life's quotidian messiness, its dreariness, complications. Walking for the first time that morning into the cafeteria at Restaurant 1, past the big four-storey conifer-something tree – he's never been strong on natural sciences – whose fallen cones disintegrate into what looks like pencil sharpenings, as if you're walking on a carpet of the residue of ideas. That first meeting with his lanyard around his neck, a bona fide postdoc researcher at CERN, seeing groups of people at the long tables scribbling on pads and gesticulating and discussing things that were unintelligible, untranslatable, probably, to almost anyone else. And that feeling – it sounds sentimental, but it was true – that everyone there was engaged in the self-same quest: to make sense of things, at the most fundamental of levels. Who we were, and what we were doing, and why – *why*.

But there is no way to convey any of that, and so he tells them a silly anecdote about walking near the collider's superconducting magnet, how its force is one hundred thousand times the strength of the earth's magnetic field, how it'll banjax your watch and wipe your credit cards if you forget to leave them at surface level, and how, if you make the mistake of wearing steel-capped boots, it's like wading through seawater.

They laugh politely this time, as they're meant to do.

And then it's time for their questions. An intense-looking boy in the front row shoots up his hand and asks a question about quantum gravity that he wouldn't be able to answer if he had a year to talk to them – a lifetime. A girl at the back, innocent-faced, asks a question about the Large Hard-on Collider, a malapropism at which her friends fall about laughing, and which both he and the principal pretend to ignore. The rest of them ask the questions that people always do. If there's a danger of a black hole that could wipe us all out. If he thinks we'll ever build a time machine. What would happen if a person got into the collider – would they be blasted to another dimension?

He tells them that black holes could be happening all the time, maybe dozens a day, but that we're in no danger because their mass cannot be larger than the energy of the photons that created them, which is negligible, at least to us. He says the collider is a sort of time machine, taking us back again and again to the Big Bang, or at least the

68

moments immediately after it. He says that a person never could, because there are six hundred interlock keys to the collider, one for every technician and physicist who needs access, and if a single one is missing, the beam won't start up. But theoretically, he says, you'd be annihilated, instantaneously, like someone chucking a lighter at a pile of fireworks, a flare of light, then – nothing.

'Well, that has certainly been a captivating hour,' the principal says, ushering him back through the sombre, familiar corridors onto the main entrance steps for a series of photographs with the head boy and head girl, with the dozen or so A-level physicists, with the intense young boy from the front row, who manoeuvres in next to him and says that he got the top mark in the entire examination board in A-level maths, taken two years early, but that it's physics he wants to study.

'So what *is* your theory for why gravity doesn't work at a quantum level?' the boy says, as the photographer arranges and rearranges the group. 'I understand,' he adds, eager, 'if you just couldn't say in front of everyone.'

'I'm afraid we just don't know,' he says.

'But what do you *think*?' the boy persists, his thin face contorted and earnest. 'I won't repeat it to anyone – just what do you *think*?'

He needs to give the boy an answer that will ignite something in him, inspire him. The sort of thing that he, at fifteen, would have wanted to hear. That maybe gravity is something that leaks in from other dimensions, where it's much stronger, places where time is warped, or slower, or in some other way unfathomably different – who knows, an actual material reality, or entirely simultaneous. He could say that maybe quantum gravity is the key to getting away from here, only for whatever reason we're not quite good enough, or ready for that yet. In this reality, so far, there's only one way out.

'I said I don't know,' he says, and he can hear the edge to his voice so tries to soften it with, 'Maybe you'll solve that one for us.'

The boy looks at him, then frowns.

A test: he's failed it.

'We have high hopes for him,' the principal says.

He can't quite face going back home – to his mother's naked shining pride, to how he'll have to lie to preserve her sense of him. So he walks for a bit, aimlessly at first – past Queen's, down Bradbury Place and Shaftesbury Square, past the Crown, the Europa, the Grand Opera House. He remembers going there as a child, to see *Postman Pat the Musical*, and of how when Pat came onstage he cried, terrified, overwhelmed, and of Kevin and Tanya laughing, his mum letting him spend the show in her lap, face crushed into her.

He turns to walk the length of May Street, towards the

Lagan. Looking across the river, he realises he's never been to the new so-called Titanic Quarter – not the quarter, nor the *Titanic* museum, not any of it. It's as good a destination as any, and then enough time will have passed that he can get a bus back across the city, and get over himself enough to smile as he tells his mum about the talk and the photographer, the principal saying it had been 'captivating', the young boy with his questions, details she'll drink in and then be telling everyone for weeks to come.

He crosses the Lagan and walks through the outskirts of Sydenham, the new Arena – the Odyssey, he thought it was called, but it's not, it's changed names even since it was new to him – and into the territory of the cranes. He has them on the tea towels in his Meyrin flat: just one of the random things that his mum is always buying and sending to him, to remind him of home.

Somewhere around here, it occurs to him, is the street named for John Bell – he read about it in one of her clippings; articles from the *Belfast Telegraph* being another thing his mum's always posting over. There'd been a bit of a to-do about it, some Belfast City Council by-law forbidding the naming of streets after people, and they'd gotten around it by naming it something else, something ridiculous-sounding . . . He finds it on his phone, sure enough, Bell's Theorem Crescent, and follows the directions. *Bell's Theorem Crescent*: the new Belfast Met building, a coffee shop, a multistorey car park. To the right, a high fence, beyond which the cranes, the wasteland to the airport.

He stands there for a bit. He should write an email, he thinks, to that boy. He could send it via the principal. Tell the boy that one of CERN's greatest-ever physicists came from Belfast, came from a working-class estate and a family too poor to send him to university, so after he left school at sixteen he became a lab technician at Queen's instead, sitting in on lectures, teaching himself mathematics and physics, gaining bachelor's degrees in both within a year. Tell him that if you want something enough, just go for it. Bell went on from Queen's to CERN, where he partially disproved Einstein, demonstrating that Einstein's views on quantum mechanics were insufficient, incorrect, though most particle physicists today believed that Bell's own theories of inequalities, of 'loopholes', must also fail. But maybe, he would write, that would be the boy's task in life, to be the boy from Belfast who built on Bell to explain quantum gravity, provided a complete and consistent theory, revolutionising physics . . .

They say John Bell was due to get the Nobel, but he died too soon – a matter of weeks. But what would it have meant anyway, a white-tie reception, some speeches, some more eponymous streets? A colleague of his, at ALPHA, has been working on one particular area of antimatter since the late eighties, a whole quarter of a century before the technology finally caught up to enable him to investigate. A year from now, two at most, that team will drop an anti-hydrogen atom, and if it deviates from the gravitational trajectory of a hydrogen atom, it will be an almost automatic Nobel Prize. If nothing different happens – well, the work has been the same, the sacrifices, the life spent the same way, and no less spent because you don't get it back. Just more meaningless, objectively.

The discovery of the Higgs had invalidated his supervisor's research, and by proxy his own – years and years of it. Overnight: meaningless. They'd been there, on the morning it was announced – not in the room itself, but on the livestream. The young Chinese American postdoc who couldn't even speak, just pointed, choked up with emotion, at the screen. It was impossible not to get a little swept up in the emotion of that day – it was rampant, surging in the ether, you might say – but as the implications of the discovery sank in, he and his supervisor and the rest of their small team had gone back to someone's office, where there was a bottle of gin and a bottle of whiskey; they'd taken turns running down to the vending machine for bottles of peach juice and cans of Coke for mixers, until none of them could be bothered moving and they'd drunk the rest of the spirits neat. His supervisor had left CERN shortly after that – just didn't have it in him to start again. He'd been lucky enough to transfer as a research assistant to the CMS, where he's been ever since.

He shivers. It's started to rain while he's been standing here – that soft, almost undetectable mizzle that will somehow have you soaked to the skin in minutes. He didn't wear a coat, because his coat's not smart enough, and his polo-neck alone is too thin. He knows he won't write the email.

That afternoon, Kevin calls over with Isla in the sling. It's the first time he's met her, which Kevin makes a big fuss about, and he does his best to play along, all the while feeling a bit ridiculous – it's not as if they have personalities at that age, and Baby Isla looks exactly the same as all three of her sisters did – as all babies do. Kevin, on the other hand, looks rounder and more jovial with every baby, the careful goatee and sideburns designed to give his face some shape, the eyes that are almost lost each time he smiles.

'Not tempted to get one of your own?' Kevin says.

'She's a wee dote,' he says.

'So, you are tempted? Ah, I'm only pulling your leg, man. Seriously, though: they change your world. Dontcha! You do – you do!' he says, dandling the baby. 'So are you seeing anyone or anything?' he throws in quickly, as if it's casual.

'Not really. Not recently.'

'You should get yourself out there, man. You're never going to meet someone in that underground man-cave of yours.'

'Very funny, Kev.'

'Shooting your big laser guns around. Come on, what are the statistics? Ninety-five per cent male?'

'Not that bad. Seventy-five per cent, maybe.'

'Jesus Christ. See, what happens,' Kevin says, 'you have daughters, and you start to realise how screwed up the world is for them. It's your job to make us a better world,' he says to Isla. 'To make yourself a better world. It is. It is! And we're only sorry we haven't done it for you. Aren't we?'

'We are,' he says. 'And we're sorry we haven't solved the problem of gravity at a quantum level.'

'But seriously, man,' Kevin says. 'It kind of sounds, don't get me wrong, but it sounds a bit solitary, your life there.'

'Sure I've my flatmate,' he says. 'She's nice.'

'Oh yeah?'

'Yeah,' he says. He doesn't say, She's gay.

'We're pretty close,' he says, and he thinks that, in some ways, they are. Sometimes when she's drunk she tells him about her dates. If one of them is cooking, and the other one is in, they eat in front of the TV together, watching the random cable shows she likes.

'Tell me more,' Kevin says.

He has never been able to make the sort of connection that Kevin means with anyone.

'No more to tell.'

'Ah here, man. I'm not being nosy. We just want you to be happy. You know how much Mum worries about you.'

'She doesn't worry about me.'

'Of course she does.'

'No more than she worries about you, or Tanya – or any of us.'

'Nah, man. Way more than that.'

Isla has begun to cry. Kevin stands, and straps her back into the complicated-looking sling, bounces her. 'Shush, now. Shush.'

'I'm fine, Kevin,' he says. 'Honestly. Seriously, I'm fine.'

'I know it's hard, now we've got, you know, death to think about.'

He looks at Kevin.

After Kevin's gone, the house feels very small and very empty. His mum is still napping.

He should tackle the boxes, he thinks.

He bags up the *Beano*s and *Dandy*s for Tanya to drive to the dump. His school reports, jotters, stapled A3 projects on space – he bags up all of them. He finds Kevin's old Soul Asylum tape, which he remembers nicking from Kevin repeatedly. He'd loved that song from it – 'Runaway Train'. The video too: he'd watched VH1 for hours on end in the hope of seeing it. All the kids in the video were actual kids who really, actually disappeared. Some turned up in the end – some, Kevin told him, because they were recognised in the video. Others never did. He had always been mesmerised by them.

He puts aside the tape to show Kev, but everything else he chucks away – the contents of box after box, six binbags' full. In a box towards the end, he finds the comics he used to draw himself, from when he was eleven, for a good couple of years – carefully tearing reams of printer paper by the perforated seams and folding it into 'books', ruled in quarters and filled with the adventures of Stick Man. He spent hours on them – hours and hours. Some days it would be all he did. He liked his HB pencils to be impeccably sharp, and so his dad bought him one of the sharpeners that clamped on to the edge of the desk, that you turned the handle of, like in school, and he'd sharpen his whole pencil tin of pencils and line them up and breathe in the shavings collected in the container's belly.

In each of his comic books, Stick Man has a breakthrough – that was the conceit. He can lower himself down into squares that haven't yet happened, or climb up into squares that have, to peer at his previous self. In one book, Stick Man discovers colour – first red, then orange, then all the rest, tumbling in a rainbow through his world, every shade in the Faber-Castell box. But every comic ends when he has to go to bed, his Stick Mother tucking him in, and things reset. He can't find it now, but he remembers drawing what must have been one of the last Stick Man books, perhaps *the* last, where he drew his own hand, drawing a doorway for Stick Man. He drew his hand life-size, 3D, as they'd been taught in art. His 3D hand and the doorway it was drawing took up the whole penultimate double-page spread. Pressed up against the bottom-left edge, Stick Man looking up – not at the doorway, but out at 'him' – wherever 'he' must be, so far beyond the scope of Stick Man's vision or understanding. The final page was Stick Man clambering through, one leg lifted, arms in the air, the back of his head, not looking back, his limbs disappearing as they went.

He always used to show his comics to his mum – would lean against the back of the armchair as she read them. He always insisted that she sat down to read them properly, not just glanced at them over the stove, or whatever it was she was doing, and she'd play into it, turning on the lamp, plumping up the cushion, sitting down with a 'Now then.' She'd read them carefully, commenting on every box, then ruffle his hair and say, 'Wee son, I'd love to know where all this comes from.'

He looks through the rest of the boxes in search of that final Stick Man comic, but it's nowhere to be found. He goes through the binbags, item by item, in case it's been tossed with other things by mistake. But it's not there either.

He is seized, then, with a sort of panic. He puts his head between his knees; tries to breathe. Out for a count of six . . .

He thinks of his dad on the day he left, clapping him on the shoulder and saying, 'Don't go making any black holes by accident', and him thinking: This entire place is a black hole – this life is a black hole. But he didn't say it because it didn't matter: he was going – in his mind's eye, faster than the observable speed of light, already gone – so far beyond this now, to the possibility of things making sense.

He used to think, he thinks, that dark matter would be the gateway to another universe – he used to think that we couldn't perceive it simply because our senses were too limited, because we'd only learned to exist in three dimensions, four at most, out of nine, eleven, twenty. He used to think that one day – one day within our life-times – we'd find a way through – to whatever adventures might be waiting on the other side. If we didn't, we were doomed: in five billion years, a slow blink on the face of deep time, the sun would swell to its 'red giant' phase, engulfing the entire orbit of Mercury, likely Venus too, leaving the earth a scorched and barren chunk of rock which would spin and spin on, before eventually shedding every last one of its atoms in the churning depths of its once solar system. He used to think that maybe dark matter was *something*, somewhere, trying to contact us, trying to tell us how to escape from this, trying to show us how to see and what to do and how to be, if only we could know it.

But now – for years now – even as he's worked on it, worked diligently, worked hard, worked overnight for night after countless night, he has secretly, dreadfully come to think that the whole theoretical concept is a red herring – a fairy tale – something we've made up to reassure ourselves, to make Einstein's theories, to make the whole Standard Model, make sense, something we're clinging to, because without it, what is there?

After a while, he sits up, cautiously. The flashing lights have faded; his normal vision stabilised. It would be too easy if the answer just came to you like that – though people do talk of it happening that way: Bell did, Einstein did, even Newton with his apple . . .

He hasn't eaten anything, he thinks, because there isn't any food worth eating in this house. He should walk to the big Forestside, buy a couple of bags' worth of vegetables, make some soup. Fresh things, green things.

Bananas, oranges. Show his mother that he's going to look after himself, and so by implication, for the next while at least, and even if she is – that he is not going anywhere.

The Counting Sheep

MARY AWAKES WITH A JOLT TO FIND THEM THERE — one, two, three, four, five, six of them, all in a row, shuffling and clopping their tiny hooves on the windowsill at the foot of the bed. She pushes aside the duvet, its stale smell of old lavender oil. Reties her loose hair, not for a moment taking her eyes off them.

One, two, three, four, five, six.

The expression on their faces is stubborn, eyes glinting with something like defiance, and not at all, she thinks, what you might call *sheepish*. *Mulish*, maybe. She kneels, edges closer. She puts out her hand, as you might to a bird, or a hamster. They are small enough that two, maybe three, could fit side by side on her palm. They shuffle, clop. Stare. One of them gives a tiny, aggressive bleat. She pulls back her hand.

They can't stay on the windowsill, that's for sure: it's a thin cracked ledge with a metre-high drop to the ground, and the flaking paint is probably toxic. Maybe, she thinks, she should sweep them up with a dustpan and throw them into the bushes outside. But something in her is reluctant:

some odd sense of duty to them, of responsibility. All night, they leapt for her round and round a yellow crescent moon, faster and faster and faster – No wonder, she says, with a not-quite giggle, yous're looking at me like that.

She gets a shoebox of bank statements and bills from the top of the wardrobe and empties it. Tilts and holds it out for them to step into, but of course they won't, and so she has to prod them, flick them almost, one by one, feeling a little more squeamish each time. She shoves the lid on the box. A chorus of bleats, like the squeak of indignant mice, but with a touch more malice. Her hands are trembling. What now?

She finds some salad for them, the last of a bag of rocket. Fills up an old ramekin with water. She lifts the lid and the six of them are huddled together in a corner.

And what, she thinks, *now*?

Mary showers, dresses. Takes off the lid once more, half-hoping they'll be gone – but they're not, and nor are the leaves and the water, which still look, in fact, to be untouched. A handful of oats? But the only oats she has are the pre-mixed sachets, Golden Syrup flavour, her Sunday-night comfort food. Straw? She has some that came in a beauty box, she thinks, and she roots about the recycling to find it, but it's synthetic straw, just paper strips. Well, the rocket leaves will have to do.

She puts the shoebox in a shady corner, where it won't

overheat. Cardboard is permeable, she thinks, so there should be air, but nevertheless she carefully makes some holes with a pencil.

There. They have food, they have water, they have air. They can't climb or gnaw, so they can't get out. Only what if, she thinks with a spike of horror, they charge at one side all at once, and it topples over, and the lid comes off, and they skitter off, everywhere, under the bed under the wardrobe into the corners into the gap under the skirting boards—

Stop it. Stopitstopitstopit.

This is how an unfettered mind wheels and plunges at 3, 4 a.m. It's a quarter past eight on a Monday morning in May now and everything will be better after a cup of coffee.

She forces herself to eat two rounds of toast as she drinks her way through a cafetière of coffee, made with so many scoops that the handle jolted and stuck as she pressed it down. She'll need another coffee come eleven, another after lunch – too much, she knows, but how else is she meant to get through the day? She gave it up for a painful six weeks, in case it was part of the problem – a fortnight of wretched headaches, and the constant feeling that she was only half-seeing the world through thick-smeared Vaseline. The next two weeks were better, at least in terms of the headaches and vision, and the last two better again – but not drinking coffee didn't make an iota of difference to her sleep, whereas drinking it did to her ability to get through a morning. She'll cut back again – she will. Next week, maybe. She'll make herself do it. She'll do bath salts and lavender and no phones in bed. She will. But not today.

It's almost a relief to have another problem to think about.

Before she leaves for the office, she checks on them one last time.

But how? she says, aloud, feeling like crying. But *how*?

One, two, three, four, five, six, stamping in one restless mass – and, darting in and out of their stubby legs, two little scraps, each barely the size of a fingernail.

Oh, Lord, she thinks. What do I do? What have I done?

She calls in sick to work.

She looks on the internet.

There is nothing to suggest how they might have gotten here, nor how she can get them to go. But wikiHow says they need grazing – seven to ten hours a day, grass and clover, alfalfa. They need salt blocks to lick, and if you don't pare their hooves they can get foot-rot, severe pain and lameness, a terrible smell. She suddenly does feel a bit sick.

There were girls in her primary school who'd be absent each year at lambing time, when their mums and dads needed to be with the pregnant ewes. By secondary school they were up lambing themselves, yawning through registration. She was always one of the ones who'd automatically, melodramatically squeal *ewwww* at the thought of sticking your hand up an animal's bum. She tries, now, to channel the pink cheeks and ponytail of someone who wouldn't be fazed by the thought of a cardboard box of procreating . . . these.

Okey-dokey, she says. Grazing.

Her wee terraced house, for all it's hers and hers alone, doesn't have a garden, only a concreted-over yard for the bins, and a front door straight onto the street. She'll have to go down Cairnburn, and hope no one sees her.

She allows herself to feel a tiny bit smug as she walks into Cairnburn, its lush expanses of grass and ample clover. Back in London, it would have been the scruffy piss-reeking patch of what passed for the local park, all scraggy pigeons flapping over discarded fried chicken boxes and chucked cider cans.

She moved home – it had never ceased being home, even if it was sometimes 'home', in quote marks, with a varying intensity of irony – six months ago, just after her thirty-third birthday, after years of her mother's newspaper cuttings about how cosmopolitan East Belfast was becoming, only to find that her parents had moved on. They were never home any more. They were *on a wee cruise*, the Hurtigruten up the Norwegian fjords, or around the

Dalmatian coast, or island-hopping in Greece. They were at their Italian class, or their life drawing, their painting lesson or their Zumba. They were having dinner at a fabulous new place in town with a couple they'd met on one of the wee cruises.

I can see you Tuesday . . . her mother would say . . . *week*. Then, swiping her finger down her iPhone's diary, Actually no, I'm having my roots done – how about the Wednesday after? Come for dinner, but it'll only be cold cuts as you know your daddy doesn't like anything sitting on his stomach when he does his yoga.

Her brother and sister-in-law have been busy too, since the twins. Mary has never wanted children herself, but she thought it might be nice to be an aunty – sweets and treats and day trips, a special, confiding, mischievous sort of a love. But the one time she looked after the girls – for less than an hour while her sister-in-law had a facial the day before the voucher expired – they came with a twelve-page document of rules and regulations, things they and she must and absolutely must not do, more complicated than many of the legal documents at work.

She saw there was a baby opera in town a couple of weeks ago, part of a children's festival, and she suggested going – it sounded nice, the soft lights and wafting gauze and opera singer, but apparently it was at the wrong time, and if the twins didn't nap then they wouldn't later, or would, or something potentially catastrophic. Give it a few years, she's told herself, till she can take them to the Pickie Funpark, or Funderland, or up the coast to Barry's, the

Mela in Botanic, and they'll be old enough to not tell their mother about minor breaches of contract like candyfloss.

But in the meantime – the squeaks from the box are getting louder – she has other charges to worry about. She finds a secluded spot, away from the main path's joggers and dog-walkers, away from the shrieks of the playground, and tilts the box gently onto its side. They're suspicious, at first, but one by one they pick their way delicately over the rim of the box and into the tall grass. She had worried, of course, that they might immediately scatter, make a break for freedom – but they don't, just set to eating.

The days pass. She takes – why not? – her annual leave, in one giddy glut. More newborns are appearing. She counts them, each morning. One, two, three, four, five six, and one, two, three, four, five, six. Seven-*eight!* She finds in the charity shop a toy farmyard, sheds and pens and barn, even a field with fences, and buys it, a change for them from the shoebox, a nicer sort of a home. But when she nudges them in, they just stand there, pressed together in one stall, as if they're not sure what they're supposed to do. Maybe they're freaked out by it – maybe to them it's unheimlich. Maybe, she thinks with a pang, they're still as bewildered to be here as I was to one day just – have them.

At night she lies there trying to summon up a cow jumping over the moon – a pig – a wee laughing dog – but it never works.

Then one morning she wakes to find things are not right. They're huddled together on the far side of the fake pond and on the other side by the fake hay-bales are two of them dead, keeled over stiff and cold, tiny ballpoint eyes unblinking.

She buries them in Cairnburn – a shallow grave scooped with her hands. Ashes to ashes, she says, dust to dust. *We all must return to whence we one day came*: the phrase, out of nowhere, floats into her head. But where might that place, for them, be? Where is it, she thinks, with a familiar, bleak edge, for any of us?

Several others are sickening now. She can sense it. And sure enough another dies, then another. Another another. Not just her nights, but her days, now, are a sick blur of panic. Eventually she puts the remaining ones into the shoebox, one, two of the originals, one, two, three of the almost-dozen newborns, this time with a handful of proper straw and a scattering of pine resin from the Templemore pet shop.

I'm sorry, she says to them. I should have done this earlier. But I was worried they'd say it was me needed a doctor.

She waits for one of them to bleat – or something – in response but of course they don't. They are still as watchful, as wary, as resentful, she can't help thinking, as they ever were.

Look, I'm sorry, she says again.

She carries the box with infinite care to the vet's.

88

In the waiting room, she rehearses in her head what to say. But when she lifts the lid – they're gone.

There's nothing there. The straw, just, dusty with resin. She lifts a handful of it out, lets it fall.

What was it in there, love? says the secretary. Was it a wee bird, was it?

She finds she can't speak.

Aye, well, the secretary says, entirely unsurprised, it's that time of year right enough, when they're just leaving the nest. That's why we say on the website, leave them in a safe place in an open shoebox, because sometimes they're just stunned, so they are, and in their own good time they up and fly away.

But, Mary says.

Nature knows best, says the secretary. That's what I always say. Mother Nature knows best, so she does.

All afternoon, all evening, there is an ache in Mary's throat, the sort she remembers from childhood, from crying.

But that night, for the first time in weeks, months, maybe even years, she sleeps a dreamless deep sleep while – who knows? – above her head the pale moons and their laughing, spinning creatures leap carelessly, obliviously by.

Openings

THE NIGHT BEFORE, you sliced your finger open halving a pomegranate. It was a deep cut: the blood welled silently, instantly, a few seconds before the pain. You held up your hand as if it wasn't your hand at all. The blood dropped and dropped. Onto the chopping board, onto the kitchen counter, onto your jeans, the floor. It needed medical attention – probably, but there was no way you were going to wake up the children, get on their shoes and coats, get you all into a taxi and to A&E, where, let's face it, the wait would be hours long. And you weren't going to call any of your in-laws. So you did your best, PAW Patrol plasters and kitchen roll, bound as tightly as you could with microporous tape. Blood was steadily seeping but not quite soaking through. Feeling foolish, and a little light-headed, you raised your hand in the air: a silent appeal to the cosmos.

The bleeding, eventually, stopped. The pain was different now: dull and aching, that first keen lustre gone. You gingerly redid the plasters and the tape, the sodden clots of kitchen roll retrieved, on second thoughts, from the bathroom pedal bin – where they might alarm your youngest, who likes to play at stamping it open and shut, lifting it up to make faces at her warped and stretched reflection on the sides – and pushed into the over-full kitchen bin. The uneaten pomegranate and the massacre of a chopping board you stood and looked at for a moment. Your mother-in-law swears by pomegranates for flawless skin – which, indeed, she has, soft and unlined – and to ensure outstanding memory, which she also has, the unerring repository of her extended family's birthdays, anniversaries, web of complex relations. She has a superstition for pomegranate too, as she has for almost everything, from itchy palms to sneezes, from not eating fish after drinking milk to not clipping your nails after dark – that you must eat every single jewel of a seed: not a single one must be left or inadvertently thrown away.

You have a deep affection for your mother-in-law: an affection that, if things weren't not so simple any more, you would easily call *love*. After each of the children was born, she cooked for you for weeks, Tupperwares of aubergine curries and chicken biryanis and tarka daal, a slow-boiled dish of lamb shank and bone marrow meant to build you back up, little pots of raita and parathas wrapped in foil. She would never knock on the door, didn't want to intrude, just left the food in plastic bags on the doorstep, and begged you not to bother washing out the containers, just to bag them back up and leave them for her to collect.

You have come home to similar deliveries in the last couple of weeks: and there's often something more too: kheer, your favourite creamy rice pudding, sprinkled with slivered almonds or pistachios and rose petals, that's meant to be made on special occasions only, and which your mother-in-law makes with rice that she grinds down to a powder first. A tub of home-made halwa or sticky gulab jamun. A string bag of half a dozen pomegranates. An acknowledgement of the birthing pains of this new life, you think, or you sometimes think it's a reminder, or a plea. You always text to thank her; she always replies with just one symbol, the hands in prayer.

You know she will be praying too – for you; for the two of you.

But it was pomegranate seeds, you thought as you looked at the mess, that bound Persephone to Hades. You shook the two halves, full and heavy as breasts, straight from the chopping board into the bin, rammed them down, with a flash of anger that surprised you even as it flared and faded.

You awkwardly undressed, then, and washed your face, brushed your teeth, got into bed, arranging your hand on a towel so it didn't bleed over the gold-threaded kantha quilt – a wedding present, but too nice to stop using, the cheering abstract patterns of it, the comforting heft.

But for the longest of times, you didn't, couldn't, sleep.

It seemed so cruel not to be able to, given that the children were: all three of them, for once. Cry when the baby cries: stamp your feet and howl when the toddler does. You'd often thought that would have been a better philosophy for new mothers. Tomorrow, the children will go to their father, as you have tried to practise thinking of him, and you'll be able, in theory, to sleep twelve hours, sixteen, if you want – to spend the whole weekend sleeping, except it never seems to work that way. You sleep even worse with them *not* nearby than with them coughing and whimpering in the room next door, as if, across the town, the invisible umbilical cords that still connect you are pulled too taut, too thin, and sing out in sorrow.

You will get used to this. All of this, you will get used to: all of you.

Eventually, you must have slept.

You wake to the children padding and scampering in, one by one, and to the overriding sound of heavy, incessant rain: another drookit day. But just one more, you tell yourself, just one more day of this: of half term, rain, of trying to entertain or at least to occupy all three without resorting to screens the entire time, and as soon as they're gone to your husband's – you say to yourself, fiercely – you'll miss them, you eejit.

Not your husband's. Their father's.

Though he is still your husband: he isn't yet not.

This day is going to be a fun day, you tell the children. We're only going to do fun things today. You eat toast with rainbow sprinkles for breakfast and then make cupcakes. You let them play their favourite game of dragging all the soft things they can find, all their bedding and even yours too, pillows and duvets and the cot mattress, sofa cushions and all of their cuddly toys, onto the floor of your bedroom to make a sort of den to roll around in, and to hurl themselves into from your bed. You let them eat their lunch – why not? – in the bathtub. Fish fingers and peas for one, fish fingers and beans for another, cheese sandwich without the cheese for the third, and two rounds of cupcakes for pudding. But there's a wild, reckless sort of energy in the air now, and they are starting to get overwrought, to squabble, to elbow and pinch each other, and first one, then all of them are crying.

The thing your mother-in-law always says is that children need a balance of treats and discipline, but mainly lots of romps to let off steam. And she should know: she raised six sons, in a terraced house no bigger than this. You've been avoiding indoor activity centres, because every time you go someone gets a new cold or bug, and after taking this whole week off work to look after them, you can't afford any more leave. But it's still raining too miserably to convince them that a rain walk would be Fun, and so you get out the phone you've promised them you won't even look at today, this Fun Day, and you book the last remaining session, which you'll just make if you leave right now, at Kidz Go Crazy!, a sort of hell on an industrial estate a short bus ride away.

Beaker and water bottles, wee-wees, raincoats and boots. Getting all three of them set to go out is like herding cats. You shout at them to line up by the door while you get yourself ready, mascara and blusher, ridiculous as it is, for a soft-play in a warehouse in the rain, in case you meet one of your husband's cousins, who might report back how haggard you looked, how you're obviously not coping. Some of them, you know, would love to see you looking rough. Some are enjoying the outrage, the scandal. Worst of all has been your husband's eldest brother's wife, also a convert, who had gone out of her way to take you under her wing. She as good as spat at you: It's not just yourself you're letting down.

Often, at times like this, when you look at yourself in the mirror, her voice replays on a loop in your head.

It wasn't just me, you try to argue back to her. But your voice is thin even inside your head.

You try to concentrate instead on the wiggle and flick of the mascara wand, the swoop of your blusher brush.

The children are jumping up and down, hanging off the latch, opening and closing the door and messing about with the snib – and when you go to leave, the front door won't open, at all. The snib slides slackly up and down without engaging or disengaging the latch.

You are locked, you realise, *in*.

Shit, you say, to the children's horror, to their delight, Oh shit, and the elder two start leaping up and down repeating it, *shitshitSHIT.*

Quiet, you say.

But, Mummy, *you* said it!

Shitshit*SHIT*, shitshit*SHIT!* even the youngest is chiming in now.

Please, you say, all of you, stop it, I need to think. We're locked in, you say, *we are locked in*, raising your voice too loud when their chanting doesn't stop.

It stops.

Like Alfie, the youngest says, uncertainly.

Like Alfie, you say, sure, but Alfie has someone to get him out – he has his mum, and Maureen, and the window cleaner with the ladder, who all know he's in there. There's no one waiting helpfully for us on the other side.

We can't get out? the youngest one says.

Ever? the middle one starts to sob, and the eldest says, gleefully, Yes, maybe we'll *die* in here, maybe we'll become *skeletons* – and this is a touchy point, your middle one having been appalled and terrified to learn this week that she has a skeleton living inside her.

Enough! you say. You jiggle the snib again, and slam the door with your shoulder, and slam the door with your shoulder whilst jiggling the snib, but it's no good.

Phone Daddy, the middle one says, and the other two take it up: Phone Daddy, and the youngest starts up with, I want Daddy!

This isn't Daddy's house any more! you snap, though, technically, it is. I'm not phoning Daddy.

But I want Daddy, rises the chorus, I want Dad-dee . . .

For a wild moment you imagine hacking at the door with a knife, the chef's knife that did for your finger yesterday, a Sabatier blade, monogrammed with your husband's initials. Instead you try a spreading knife, blunt and useless, wiggling it ineffectually between the door and jamb. The effort has reopened the cut on your finger: the blood is seeping again. *Fuck.*

Why won't you call Daddy? the eldest asks.

Because I can't.

Why not?

You don't reply. You *could* call your husband. He'd come round as soon as he could, you know he would, and he'd somehow make you all laugh about it. He'd call a cousin who could help with the lock and he'd banter with them as they worked, easy and charming, his thick-lashed puppy-dog eyes, the baby of his family, the clown. He would make everything ok.

But you can't keep calling him: not for every little thing.

Ok, you say. I have a plan.

But we've missed the soft-play, your middle child sobs. This isn't a fun day, this is the worst day ever.

No, you say. This is a Fun Day, it's definitely a Fun Day. And guess what? We're all going to climb out through the living room window, like burglars in reverse. Come on! This isn't just a Fun Day, it's an Adventure too.

But the pumpkins, your eldest says, and it's true, you arranged the pumpkins you'd carved at the start of half term on the outer ledge of the window, four heads in a row, leering and grinning.

Never mind the pumpkins, you say, and you try to take a breath and smile as you say it. Sure we took photos of the pumpkins, didn't we?

They'd wanted to show their dad the pumpkins, asked you to take and send a picture, *insisted* you did. You did: cautiously. You haven't yet established how this works; the tone to take. It gives you such a particular, peculiar ache when he texts dutiful blurry photos of them on swings at the playground, or when you see his face at the start of a bedtime video call. So you just texted the picture and messaged, *Carving Pumpkins!*, to which he responded with the thumbs-up reaction, all-round false cheer.

When, you think, did you lose the habit of tenderness with each other, of restraint and consideration and respect? How did it somehow seep away into what it so wretchedly, then irrevocably, seemed to become: first arguing in whispers, after the children were asleep, and then when they were in a different room, and finally just yelling at each other, yelling and sobbing like children yourselves, and over what? Money, of course, but also things like the stacking of the dishwasher or the division of domestic chores, that weren't things at all, except that of course they were, they were just other things.

And the stupid, ironic twist is that you've been polite with each other recently, careful, calm, and you've started to see how you were together, how you worked together, how you were a team, and a good one, for so long.

But now it's just you and the children crying and so you heave the window outwards and the four pumpkins splat wetly onto the ground, mushily shattering.

Oh well, you say brightly, you'll be with Daddy and Uncle Yusuf and Aunty Amira and your cousins for

Hallowe'en, I'm sure you'll carve more then, even better ones, and you clamber out of the window.

And Kidz Go Crazy! – you and your husband used to joke – does exactly what it says on the tin. All is forgotten and they hurtle round, hurling balls, playing tag, driving Little Tikes cars into each other.

You shift your table to allow a woman with a tray of slushies and chips to squeeze in next to you. There is a green sticker on the table's rim: *Families that Pray Together*, it says in a bubbly font, *Stay Together!* Someone has attempted, ineffectually, to pick it off. You wonder what you failed to centre in your lives, to revere. You wonder if you'll ever find it now.

The imam who took the classes before you got married said to always check your heart's intentions: that what God looks at is the purity of the heart's intentions. Nothing else matters, he said: this is all. As he said it, you felt something loosen in your chest, the grip of some terrible vice, that you realised must have been there most of your life: the almost-certainty of damnation. From that moment on, you were glad to convert: you didn't just do it for appearances, or because it was expected of you. It simply made sense. It still does. Even at the price of all it slammed shut between you and your parents, with whom you talk now only warily, and only ever about the children, and to whom you haven't yet brought up any of this; and between you and your sister, who escaped your upbringing in other, more straightforwardly rebellious ways.

But the mess of it all is that through all this you've only been intending to do the right thing, or at least the less-wrong thing; for the children, yes, but for yourself too, for both of you, because things had become untenable.

You think of the silence in the moments after you finally used that word.

Thank fuck it's Friday, says the woman who's just squeezed in. Kylie! Brendan! Get over here. Seriously, thank fuck!

Ha, you say, not sure if she's talking to you, or just herself, but she smiles and rolls her eyes at you.

Two hours from now, the kids'll be at my mum's, and I'll be like: part-ay.

Fri-yay! you say.

Fucking right. Friyay – Friyay! she chants, pumping the air with the palms of her hands.

That Friday feeling, of the end of half term finally in sight, is palpable. Two toddlers run slap-bang into each other, a head-on collision, like a comedy sketch, and fall apart roaring. Two adults rush to pick them up. Somewhere else, a child is shrieking, whether in pleasure or outrage, impossible to say. A pack of pre-teen girls are crashing round in circuits, chucking balls from the ball pit at each other, lurching into smaller children, empty chairs. You get up and marshal your own, pink-cheeked and damp-haired, over-exerted, over-stimulated, and say it's time to go, and they protest, run off, begin to beg, belligerently and variously, for pound coins for the claw-crane machine, for dinner here instead, blue slushies and chips, please, they all band together, *Pleeease*. No, you start to say, automatically, you've already had so much sugar today, think of the rainbow sprinkles, think of the cupcakes, come on, shoes and coats; but a tiny anarchic part of you thinks, Oh screw it, why not? and so, Ok, you say, and they blink in surprise before yelling and grabbing at each other and pogoing about with joy.

Back home, through the living room window, and already paying the price of the slushies: all three grizzling and fighting. It's later than you'd intended to be out, in fact it's almost bedtime, but – you remember with a sinking feeling – you have to sort out all the bedding and pillows before you can even open negotiations.

Would you like a film? you say, hurriedly qualifying it with, Not a whole one, just half an hour, and before a new round of bickering can break out over which, you've found and put on *The Lion King*.

Up to the bit where Simba escapes, ok?

You press play, and watch them for a moment, sprawled and curled on the sofa. You think of how, when they're born so entire and unfeasible, so miraculously unlikely, it seems impossible that you ever could raise your voice to them. You have framed photographs on the mantelpiece of each of them as a newborn, photos you printed and framed the day after their father left, *because* their father left, because you wanted the joy to be evident to them, your exhausted shining faces in their blue-and-white hospital caps cheek to cheek with each of theirs, crumpled, wrinkled, mere minutes old. You think of that first, emergency, Caesarean, the astonishing, obliterating pain that preceded it, and of the later elective C-sections, the intimate knowledge of all that was to come. You think of how you packed the hospital bags together, nappies and pads and muslins and clothes, breast pads and Lansinoh, peppermint teabags and snacks, and how your husband had raided the Mars Bars before you'd even reached the hospital, and you'd laughed till you'd actually wet yourself, and you think, it will be impossible to ever have that closeness with someone again, the purity of that connection, and then you think: No, you mustn't think like that.

You go into the kitchen and pour a glass of water, drink it by the sink. The lunch things, the baking things, the breakfast things, even last night's bloody chopping board, are still piled in there.

Five minutes, you think.

You sit down and scroll through your phone's notifications, your social media.

Your sister is having posh drinks with her friends in a bar: in the selfie she sent, her face is smooshed up against the electric-pink glass of what is clearly not the first cocktail, beaming.

A friend's play, which was forced to close early, is being revived: is going, in fact, on a short regional tour ahead of a whole new West End life. *Champers all round, dahling!!* his post says.

The boots that you ordered in an online sale, for a fantasy wardrobe that you will end up returning, because you can't spend money on boots now, have just been dispatched.

A dolphin has killed itself by closing its blowhole, a few months after it lost the human it loved, when that specific research project into fertility in captivity was decommissioned. Dolphin suicide: what a world.

You confirm that the delivery, if you're not in, can be left in your Safe Place. You text back your sister: *Cheers!* and the martini glass. You text back your friend: *Congratulations, that's amazing, hurray for you!* and the champagne glasses clinking. Then, on a whim, you open the fridge and take out a bottle of beer for yourself. You didn't mind giving up alcohol – you'd never had much of a taste for it anyway, hated the peer pressure at uni to do shots – but your husband likes an occasional beer with the football, and there are a few left in the fridge.

And fuck it, you say out loud, it's Friyay.

You prise off the cap: raise the bottle.

What are you drinking to?

A Friday full of blessings and openings, your husband used to say to you every Friday morning, in the voice you loved and then lately couldn't bear: playful, ironic, meaning it, but always ready to backtrack if anyone suggested he was being serious; always on the verge of being an impression of himself.

Khair o barkhat, you'd say back, as you'd learned the phrase for Friday blessings more properly was, because his wasn't even a real phrase, just something he'd picked up somewhere, or made up.

But now you think: To openings. To that poor bloody dolphin. To a better life. Even if just imagined. To this one. To everyone's happiness, everywhere, and to the possibility of being happy for others – your sister, your friend, the woman from the soft-play on her night out – you try the thought out, and for a moment it almost works. A sort of flickering of the synapses. Neurons that fire together, wire together. Happiness is a state of mind. Happiness is a habit. The deepest wellspring of happiness is the habit of gratitude. You close your eyes. You haven't yet drunk from the bottle. You realise that you don't particularly want to. You try to scrutinise your heart, to see if it's humble, to see if it's pure. Help me, you say in your heart, help me to get through these days – these days of which the most that will ever be able to be said is that you got through them: you got through.

Daylight Raids

In a half-ruined house, they are smoking.

Look. Look closely: can you see them?

There he stands, his uniform, blue serge with red piping, smeared with soot, the silver buttons dull – all but the one that she touched with her thumb when they met; rubbed in a slow circle clear. His tin hat in his hand. His belt with its spanner and axe. His sandy hair, its glint of red, is damp, still shows the marks of the teeth of the comb: he dunked his head and washed his face in a basin back at the station, before coming to meet her. He's been on duty for forty-eight hours, and now it's his break: twenty-four hours off. He is exhausted, but it's almost impossible to sleep right after a shift. Most of the other auxiliaries have headed to Soho, to bars with deep cellars, to drink themselves blind, but he managed to telephone a message to her to meet him, by the Baker Street side of Regent's Park, because he wanted—

But look, oh look . . . He is laughing. She has said something unexpected or maybe unintentionally amusing, and it has made him laugh. Self-conscious now, she stands a little straighter. Her dark-blue uniform coat and skirt, tie tight at her throat; her own tin hat and hand-bell neat at her feet.

A looking-glass on the mahogany bureau is swinging almost imperceptibly; the liquid tilt of it.

I'm sorry, he says, you know I didn't mean— and then he says, Oh Constance, and there is something in the way he says it that makes her turn to look at him.

Constance, he says again. *Constance*, though to everyone apart from her mother she's always been *Connie*, and even to her mother it's usually *Ohconstancedear*, one heaved long-suffering breath.

She looks at him, brown eyes frank. She is weighing up what to say, and how, and maybe whether or not to say it.

(Do you think they can feel us, watching? I don't think they can, they are too intent on each other. I think it's about to happen, this *something* that's been so long building, welling up, until it can't be carefully ignored any longer.)

But now a tremor. The shuddering feeling of something being ripped, groaning apart. A dusting of plaster descends. They look up to the ceiling. The blind mouth of a light fitting, where a chandelier must have hung. The intricate grapes and coiled vines still mainly intact on the coving.

Are we safe? she says, and then laughs, because they aren't, as no one is, and what is it girls say to soldiers in cafes and bars? *Would you die in my arms tonight, darling?*

Still: impossible to believe it will be *you* who dies. Not now. Not yet.

She bends quickly to stub out her cigarette in a chunk

of brick. (She can't bring herself to stub a cigarette out on the parquet floor, even in a house that's surely condemned.) He simply flicks his over the edge.

For the whole front wall of this house – I haven't yet told you this – is missing: collapsed, obliterated, simply gone. The ground floor is a mass of rubble, the first-floor balcony and Juliet doors destroyed, the wall itself a window now out onto the city, the night. He noticed it last night – or was it the night before? – racing past the stately curve of the terrace on the way to another conflagration, and immediately thought he had to bring her here. The aerial bombardment of London, not yet termed by the popular press *the blitzkreig*, is still in its early days, and a house like this a novelty: a doll's house with the hinged front removed, a stage set held together for barely much longer, and only for them. Clambering over chunks of fallen masonry and up what remains of the staircase, soft treacherous heaps of crumbling plaster, so slippery underfoot, glass splinters, and everywhere black dust, so they could look out unimpeded over Regent's Park.

Some person or persons unknown – the owners, perhaps, or more likely the people they employ – have been here already; uselessly begun to sweep the worst of the dust and debris to the room's edges, then abandoned the broom. The room has been stripped, too, by inhabitants – or opportunists – of any silver, any glassware or china that survived the blast, and most of its movable possessions. What remains: some sodden books. A chaise-longue, also sodden. A wall-mounted clock, fallen to the floor, casing shattered, decorative eagle's wing snapped in half. A scuttle of coal, upended. The wind has blown in, and last night's rain. Already signs of colonisation by intrepid or foolish pigeons, driven from their roosts in the park by the bombs. Their spattered shit. An occasional feather.

Another tremor: stronger this time. Something above – or below, impossible to tell – on the verge of being rent asunder. The awful sensation that it is the house itself moaning in pain.

We haven't got much longer, he says, just as she says, We should go.

But they don't go. Instead, they take one more step towards the very edge, brick dust and splintered wood, and for a moment they stand there.

They haven't touched each other, yet. Can you feel this? I think you can feel it, watching them. (When they do, he will wonder at how warm she feels, at how she seems nearly to pour into his arms, something long held back, some floodgate lifting; and she at how steady his arms feel, how solid, familiar. The scar on his forearm she remembers from when they were children, the fall from the stable roof, a thin, tight-white seam, which she will trace with her fingertip as if she could undo him – as if, she'll think, they're not both already undone.)

But all of that, if they get out in time, if they survive the night, is still ahead of them. For the moment, just look.

In the twilight, the deserted park is otherworldly, the empty boating lake, the rows of empty deckchairs, the silent, implacable trees.

Never forget this, he says, turning to her. He takes off his spectacles and presses his eyes, red-rimmed with soot and grit and tears, with the heels of his hands, blinks rapidly, presses hard again, as if he can clear them of all they have seen to see only this, now. And her: and her.

Constance, he says, softly.

I promise, she says.

Here we are. They stand.

What are they thinking? As they stand there, what are they each, both, thinking?

I wonder if Robert – that's his name, by the way, and with a childhood best friend known as Bobby, no one has ever called him anything else – I wonder if Robert is thinking this. There is a poem by a ninth-century monk, whose name is lost to us, written in the uppermost margin of a manuscript now in the monastery of St Gall, in Switzerland, but likely compiled in a scriptorium in Nendrum, on the Ards Peninsula. You'll know it: *The wind is rough tonight / Tossing the white-combed ocean. / I need not fear fierce Vikings / Crossing the Irish Sea . . .* The poem would be familiar to Robert too, because he's part Irish on his mother's side; spent boyhood holidays with his great-aunt and uncle on the Bangor coast; is sure to have visited Nendrum, scrambled about the ruins, scraped knees and freckles, making a visor of his hands to look out over Strangford Lough, half-pretending to scour the horizon for longboats.

I think he thinks of it now, as he gazes over Regent's Park at the falling dusk. Everything happening at once, or about to. Even here, standing so close to Constance that his sleeve is only just not brushing hers, I think he has the impulse that I do, that you have, half instinct, half compulsion, to work out how to say it, *this*.

The skies are calm tonight . . . If, he thinks, if he can only get the words right, the spell will preserve them, keep them safe, here, for tonight and always. *Over this moon-carved —* yes, he thinks — *this moon-carved city*.

And Constance?

Maybe she's thinking that if she were telling their story she would not set it on a precipitous ledge in a building about to fall down. She is calm, Constance, like her name; she is steady, practical — or at least she always has been. Maybe that's what she's thinking: about the way she's always been, or seen herself, or wanted to be.

I am holding them there as long as I can, you see, holding time still, this window open. I am willing time, for as long as possible, to be away and somewhere else . . . To give them this moment—

But listen. A sudden, eerie, plucked-string twang, rapidly coalescing into the rise-and-falling banshee wail of the air raid siren.

They start; look at each other. They'd been sure the Germans wouldn't come tonight. Everyone's been saying it, all afternoon. The skies are too clear, the moon will be too full. The blackout is futile on a night like this: everything visible above, and for miles, but the Luftwaffe planes are vulnerable too, forced upwards by the steel-tethered barrage balloons into the range of the ack-ack guns, silhouetted against the sky, the rising harvest moon.

Come on, he says. We're not going to die tonight, neither of us. But we do have to get out of here.

Let me get my torch ready, she says, briskly, the ARP warden in her taking over. She passes him her hand-bell, held so its tongue is stilled – Do you mind? I'll need a free hand. Puts on her tin hat. Checks the whistle on its string around her neck. Takes the torch from her pocket, though doesn't yet switch it on.

Alright, she says. I'll go first.

They will survive the night. She'll make it through the sandbagged streets to her sector post, and through the endless horrors of the hours, seeking the wounded amongst the scorching wreckage, under the roaring red-gold of the skies, under the searchlights clustering then sweeping apart, amidst the grime and chaos of the shattered streets, dressing wounds by torchlight, improvising tourniquets, until the ambulances come. He'll join a human chain of rescuers attempting to help a family trapped in a cellar by a burst water main. The grandmother and her son and his youngest child will survive: the wife and other three children will not. After that he'll go to the Hungaria on Lower Regent Street, its deep cellar, its water- and gas-proof doors, to drink himself into a stupor, pass out. In the morning, they'll each make their separate way to their separate homes through blazing, unfamiliar streets, some still tinkling with the sound of falling glass. Dustcarts abandoned where their horses have been hastily unhitched from the shafts. Piles of litter, heaps of rubble, smouldering timber, charred broken bricks. The choking, acrid smoke; eyes stinging, lungs heaving. His bedsitter will still be intact, and her house too, though the windows in the entire street will be blown in and the rooms full of soot and dirt and glass, despite the carpets Henry nailed to the frames to protect them.

The house by Regent's Park, as Robert will see the next evening, detouring there on his way to report to his station, will be entirely destroyed, of course; collapsed entirely in on itself: a toothless gape now in the creamy smile of the terrace. *What will it mean*, he'll scrawl in his notebook, the splayed old nib of his fountain pen spattering ink, *that we were there – here?*

The other characters in this story.

There's Henry, Constance's husband, who works at Senate House, newly the Ministry of Information. (She has visited him there on occasion: the almost perversely complicated lift system and long warren of corridors, where, she thought, you expected to see rows of chairs with invalids under tartan rugs, as if on the deck of some ocean-going liner. Henry's office, windowpanes removed as a precautionary measure, cloth fixed over the frames; the dim light, the draughtiness. The incongruous, oversized walnut desk, commandeered from another life entirely. The blackboard, still dusty with half-wiped chalk: equations of some other reckoning, a time when things could still be expected, reasonably, to balance.)

Henry is the moral compass of this story. Henry does not want to be in London during the war. Henry does not want there to be a war. Henry is a pacifist, though too dutiful to be a conscientious objector: a childhood illness, rheumatic fever, left him with a weak heart and occasional shortness of breath: he could not pass the army's medical.

Henry is kind. Henry is dutiful. Henry is devoted. Though it could never be said he's impulsive, Henry thinks and feels things deeply, carefully. Henry grew up with chocolate Labradors, Rollo and Duke and Brownie and Prince, and he reminds Constance of one himself, at times; his willingness, his hopefulness. She loves Henry. She loves him. She does. She made promises to him in the quiet, dusty beeswax nave of her little parish church that she intended, still does intend, to keep. The warmth of his hands. How steady his eyes are. When she thinks of it, she aches with love for him.

Also here, though at the periphery: their two boys, Harry and Ned, eight and six (or if you ask them: practically nine and nearly seven), in Hampshire these last few months with Henry's bustling, capable mother, in her element, it seems, when it comes to turning the front lawn over to vegetables, organising tea parties and country walks for evacuees, the boiling and preservation of gallons of surplus fruit, knitting circles.

And Constance's brother Bobby, killed in action this summer in North Africa (the telegram boy with his satchel at the gate, then coming down the driveway, then at the door, and the little buff card, *The Air Ministry regrets to announce* . . . the boy still waiting, Constance's mother managing to get the words out, No, no reply, thank you, no reply, and his reply to that, a bob of the head, a muttered, embarrassed, *I'm sorry, Mam*).

We should pause at Bobby. In a way, he's the most important of all: the link between Robert and Constance, their point of connection, communion. The memorial service, that bright warm day, the sandwiches on the lawn and cups and cups of tea, the farce of it, the unreality, as if it wasn't, shouldn't, really be true, as if Bobby, the real, live Bobby, lopsided grin and tanned thin face and dark unruly hair, would walk in, kitbag over shoulder, couldn't help but be summoned by the force of their longing, I say, they've gone and made an awful balls-up, of course I'm not bloody dead, how could I be? Every voice half-heard his, every movement caught in the corner of the eye, because it would be just like him, wouldn't it, to turn up at his own funeral, the prank of it, just like him. And then: Robert, did you say? Not the Robert who— Ohconstancedear! Do you remember—

And goodness, yes! she said, she did.

And she does: when Robert lived almost next door to them, the second of the three stone cottages that backed onto the

114

meadowside lane. The games the boys would have, which Constance mostly disdained, only a tiny part longed to join in. Trapping newts in the long-pond; jam jars and nets and the green smell of pondweed, the mud cool and thick on your toes. The adder they found in the meadow that time, brought home on the end of a stick. The sheep's skull, blotchy and yellowly gleaming, that marked the entrance to their domain, a crawl space under the rhododendron where they stashed broken biscuits and bottles of Tizer; painted stripes on their faces with a piece of charred cork. If she was eleven, they would have been eight: skinny arms flung around each other's shoulders, heads tilted conspiratorially, shoulder blades jutting and pale.

Did she race Robert, once, across the lawn, just to prove she could win, and did she once climb higher than either of them in the old horse chestnut tree? Did they dare her, once, at dusk, to take off her dress and her petticoat and swim in the pond, and did she do it, did she take off her vest and knickers too?

If the boys were older, perhaps, she would remember; as it was, they were just an annoying jumble of jokes and japes and limbs, when she was starting to experiment with pinning her hair in a coil rather than her two plaits, to help her mother with the flower arrangements for supper parties, to wear longer skirts. Thirteen and ten; fifteen and twelve; by then the years an unbreachable gap. A memory of the boys setting off for boarding school, freshly initialled trunks loaded into the motorcar. Her own mother, fussing about and issuing orders; Robert's mother anxious and thin, turning to press away tears; the shameful feeling of having noticed that. Bobby tall and tanned like a young Grecian god; Robert blinking behind his spectacles, not yet in any respects caught up. And sometime then – when would it have been? – the death of his father. A few months later, a year? In her memories, it barely registers. So many people have died now, and since, so many hundreds upon hundreds. Robert's mother must have moved away, because she remembers the new people moving in to the cottage: the man kept racing pigeons in a coop he built in the garden, and took her and Bobby to see them; the soft, bumbling coo of them, their rolling eyes.

Did she ever see Robert again? He was never one of the boys Bobby brought home in the long vac or for exeats, so far as she can remember, so most likely not. But she'd never given him any more thought until that moment (*Robert, did you say? Not the Robert who— Ohconstancedear!*) and the sudden relief, the sickening relief, of those precious few minutes that followed. *That time you dared each other to balance on the stable roof, I say, do you know, I still have the scar, You don't, I promise you, I do!* And then, all too soon, a motorcar leaving for the station, the prospect of a compli-cated journey back, and duties to report for – *Must you go? I'm afraid I must, but look here, I'll look you up and we can meet in London. Alright then,* she says, and then, as he walks up the lawn, and away, *Drive safely,* she hears herself calling, as if something in her knows, or fears, already.

It's winter now, there as here. The Indian summer has passed, and autumn, and winter's set in, dank and unyielding. Blue mist on the fields in Hampshire, when Henry manages to borrow a motorcar and barter some petrol, and they drive down to see the boys. The boys, so far as Constance can tell, are happy: showing off the vegetable beds they helped to turn and weed, the frost on the tough outer leaves of the brassicas, the gnarly rind of the winter squash. The wire they helped dig two yards into the ground around the chicken coop, to keep the chickens from the dog-fox seen at dusk. Collecting the last of the beechnuts, filling their satchels to take to the farmer, for sixpence apiece, for his pigs. Ned seems to have grown an inch more: he's as tall as Harry now. And both boys have grown up in other ways: they no longer hurtle towards her, yelping and jumping like puppies, but greet her instead with their new sense of responsibility, Harry (rapidly copied by Ned) offering a hand for her to shake. (Hello, Mother, hello, Mother, then Harry again, quickly, not to be outdone, How d'you do.) Oh Harry! Ned! She loves them and she yearns for them, her boys, and when she's with them she's overcome with a rush of having missed them, so forceful it's almost a physical pain. But the truth is that, back in London, the boys somehow cease to exist: all else so provisional, the world they inhabit, or even the possibility of it, once again impossible to imagine.

London. There is nothing glamorous about living in a war zone: the dreadful grind of it. The propaganda reels they show in the picture-houses, stoic people grinning, pouring cups of tea: it's lies, all of it. London is sheer abject terror coupled with boredom; the sense of time having abandoned you. The queues of people, mostly women and children, that start to form in the streets outside the public air raid shelters from midday on, clutching bags and quilts, blank-faced. Unnatural to see so many children sitting, not skipping about, or playing. The lines of old ladies waiting to buy groceries, and then you see they're not elderly at all, just stooped and exhausted, faces under their headscarves lined and creased with dust. New mothers trying to warm a bottle for a starving baby – no gas, since the mains were hit – over the naked flame of a roadman's lamp. The stultifying, choking air of a public shelter in an Underground station: the metal bunks, the stained and stinking bundles of sheets, soiled by other people's vomit or urine. The thin, insistent noise of babies crying. Children squabbling, mothers snapping. The psychotic babbling of the distressed elderly, or unhinged. Trying to block your ears with twists of cotton wool and sleep. No sleep. For nights on end, no sleep. The mournful howl of the all-clear, and stumbling home through defamiliarised streets, the sandbags, the fires, the smoke, the buses toppled into craters, the collapse of damaged buildings right before you in a sudden and terrible rush. The dust, the glass, the piles of litter in the street, the burst water mains, the stench, the soot. The emboldened vermin – the cockroaches. The never being clean. The dust and grit in your eyes, on your tongue, under, it seems, your very skin. Sponging and pressing your uniform each morning to wear again that night, the acrid smell you can never eradicate, the rising tide of body odour from the damp stained armpits as soon as you put it back on.

And night after night: the sirens, the bombs. The drone of the enemy planes and the shattering bursts of the anti-aircraft guns. The whistling plunging whine of the HEs and the whoosh of incendiaries catching. The blinding boom of the parachute mines, the reverberations going through your very marrow. The bodies in the street, some hurriedly shrouded, some not, some missing limbs, some with their faces twisted up in horror, or bemusement. After the initial thrill of the terror – the relief of something so long-awaited and dreaded finally happening, of the worst having come to pass and still being here – the quickening, sickening guilt too – what now, what now, what next?

Why does Constance stay in London? Henry would like her to be with the boys; Henry would leave London too, if he could. She knows she should leave. Unlike so many wretched others, for whom there isn't a choice, she can, and she should. But she stays. Something is in motion now, she knows, and she has to see it through. In every other world but this, she is a respectable thirty-two-year-old wife, and capable mother of two. She had never so much as imagined she might be someone else, or different.

And Robert? It's a terrible thing to say, but the war – and it *has* – has made him feel alive, or alive again. Who, after all, is he, and at twenty-nine what has he done with his life? A failed aspiring poet, reject of the air force on account of his near-sightedness (bane of his childhood, bane of his life), perennial disappointment to his mother, with his countless new starts, endless schemes. Insomniac. But nothing matters any more, and so suddenly everything might. The feeling of having no past, no future, just this moment now, and this, and this, is an awful, quickening thing. Time, or one's sense of it, is speeded dreadfully, giddily up. Each night, every hour, again and again, might well be the last you have: and so how are you going to spend it? The auxiliary firemen are heroes now. They do things that just a few months ago even the official fire brigade might have shied away from. Nightly, they cross the line between life and almost certain death, and back again. Again and again. Slipped from all moorings, anything feels, might even be, possible.

A lot has happened since we last saw Robert and Constance together. Thousands of people have died, thousands and thousands, hundreds each night.

From the *Manchester Guardian*: *Children sleeping in perambulators and mothers with babies in their arms were killed when a bomb exploded on a crowded shelter in an East End district during Saturday night's raids. By what is described as 'a million-to-one chance' the bomb fell directly on to a ventilator shaft measuring only about three feet by one foot. It was the only vulnerable place in a powerfully protected underground shelter accommodating over 1,000 people . . .*

The bombs seem not to fall or even rain so much as rush down in their zeal to annihilate. Here's Virginia Woolf: *Oh*

*I try to imagine how one's killed by a bomb. I've got it fairly vivid
– the sensation: but can't see anything but suffocating nonentity
following after. I shall think – oh I wanted another 10 years – not
this – and shan't, for once, be able to describe it. It – I mean death;
no, the scrunching and scrambling, the crushing of my bone shade
in on my very active eye and brain: the process of putting out the
light – painful? Yes. Terrifying. I suppose so. Then a swoon; a
drain; two or three gulps attempting consciousness – and then dot
dot dot.*

It's been hard to find Constance and Robert in the chaos
of these shattered days. I've spent hours trawling through
old newspapers online and in libraries on microfiche, maps
of bomb damage, weather reports, trying to see where they
might be and what they've been doing. I've read and reread
writers of the time, their novels, their diaries, for clues.
Their clothes. Their meals. Their likely duties. Anything.
Archives of oral accounts of the Blitz, still just about within
living memory. Sometimes I think I've lost them. Then I
find them again in the unlikeliest of places. Like here: a
ghost story from a Mercier Press collection, found one
afternoon in a charity shop on the Charing Cross Road,
which goes like this:

A nobleman, a wild and feckless man. One evening, a
mysterious carriage draws up to his door, and a stranger asks
to see him. He receives the stranger in his study, whereupon
they converse at length, after which the stranger departs as
abruptly as he arrived. Whatever he's said has a profound
effect on the nobleman, who immediately changes his ways,
and for some months lives the life of a reformed and

penitent man. But the lure of his former friends and carous-
ing prove too much, and he slips back into old habits. On
the anniversary of the stranger's visit, his servants note that
he is preoccupied and jumpy, despite the revels in the ban-
queting hall. Outside it is stormy, but at midnight, over the
sound of the wind and the rain, can be heard horses' hooves
in the driveway and the clatter of wheels in the courtyard.
The mysterious stranger is back. He stalks into the study, and
the guests watch as he draws the outline of a ship on the
wall. The outline, they later swear, then seems to somehow
detach itself from the wall and the ship grow solid; the
stranger climbs inside it and the nobleman follows, without
a struggle. The ship sails into the wall, and disappears, and
neither man is ever seen again.

In the gloaming of his bedsitter, you see, and I realise this
as I read it, my own London blurring, the hairs on the back
of my neck rising, Robert is telling this story to Constance.
It is barely four o'clock, there as here, but there as here
already almost fully dark outside, and inside too, with no
lamps lit, even without the blackout blinds in place. The
kettle cold beside the gas ring, their cups of barely touched
coffee (or what passes for it) cold. They are lying on the
divan; Constance has not yet redone her hair.

It's a true story, Robert is saying, though he's half-smiling
as he says it.

And why not believe it? she says, her face calm and
serious. She has never, in her life, expected to believe in
such things, but there is so much of her life, now, that she
has never expected.

Robert's fingertips, tracing down the bend of her elbow, inner arm and wrist and open palm and round and slowly up again.

Don't stop, she says suddenly.

Not ever.

Another while, for them, passes.

She will go now, she must. Even if the buses are running, it will take her the best part of two hours to get back to Clapham. To check their own blackout blinds, to heat up whatever meal the char-woman has left. To bathe and sponge down her uniform. (She has taken to wearing trousers, rather than a skirt, and flat-heeled shoes. The liberating feeling of no scratchy stockings, or having to worry about darning them again.)

She must make it look as if she came straight home, after her shift, rather than to Soho, here. That she's been at home all day, and if Henry couldn't get through on the telephone, then it must have been a fault on the exchange, or maybe she was sleeping.

I really must go, she forces herself to say.

Robert reaches across her for the tin on the side table and taps out a cigarette. The flare of the match and the hiss and crackle as the cigarette catches. He inhales, passes it to her. Exhales. She inhales, exhales, too.

Would you— she says, and she stops.

Go on, he says, but she shakes her head, no: it's silly.

Go on, he says again, but she is sitting up now, reaching behind and beginning to retwist and pin her hair. He watches her hands; the deft, unselfconscious movements.

She feels for stray hairs, smooths the sides. He loves her hands.

I would, he says.

You don't know what I'm asking, she says.

Oh, he says. I do.

Oh yes: this is a ghost story too. Maybe all loves, all lives, are haunted by what they've never quite been, or managed to become.

The fact that they are fictional – I know you'll know this – doesn't make them any less real. Robert and Constance, Constance and Robert. After that glimpse of the bedsitter, the vision, or rather the *sense* of them there, stays with me for days.

December. Oh, December.

And then the new year: day breaks on January 1st, and London is burning. Several churches have been destroyed overnight, and the Guildhall. So many great old buildings smashed; grand squares in ruins. Everywhere, devastation. A typhoid outbreak in the East End slums. To compound the misery, pneumonia rife. The death toll unimaginable. How long can this go on? But it does go on.

Robert's duty roster, Constance's rota, Henry. Rarely do the three align to allow them any window of time at all.

But yet they manage it. A quick walk through a park, or a cup of tea at a Lyons, but mostly, these days, his Soho bed-sitter, where here they are again, both just off-duty. They don't ask each other about resolutions. They don't ask what 1941 might bring. Instead, How is it you know, she's asked him, so exactly what it is that I want? and he's kissed her bare shoulder and lifted a handful of hair to kiss her neck and replied: I could not find you more irresistible if I tried.

Here's a question for you, Mr Writer, she says then.

He smiles, gestures with his cigarette: Go ahead.

(The smoking seems overdone, I know, at least to us, but it is what they do, almost constantly; a nervous habit, a comfort, a prop; even Constance, who knows that Henry loathes the smell of cigarette smoke on her breath.)

Why, she says, is *more irresistible* so much stronger than *less resistible*?

He takes a drag. I'd say, he says. (Plumes smoke.) I'd say . . . when you hear *less resistible*, all you hear is *resist*, with the sense of diminishment already provided, or fore-shadowed, by *less*. With *more irresistible*, on the other hand, not only do you have the surging effect of *more*, you somehow hear or feel most the prefix—

She is softly laughing now, but he, though he began facetiously, is suddenly serious.

Ir-, he says, a rather powerful prefix, most commonly *in-*, which in front of *l* changes to *il-*, in front of *b*, *m* or *p* becomes *im-*, and slips to *ir-* of course before *r* – and which somehow means not just *not* or *without* – inability, illogical, irrefutable – but also *in* and *into* – illuminated, immensity, inamorata – sweeping you as forcefully on as the word as a whole suggests.

I love you, she says. Then she turns and reaches blindly, in sudden agitation, for an ashtray, mashes her cigarette out. Christ, she says. Oh *fuck*.

I love you too, he says.

For a moment neither of them moves.

Constance, he says, quietly. I could give you all that I am, have, could ever be, and it wouldn't make a difference, would it.

For a long while she says nothing. Then, finally, My love, she says.

That evening, in her diary: *We live*, Constance writes, *with our noses pressed against a closed door.* In this city without windows, it is impossible even to conceive of a future. But how does this end? she wants to ask. Just how does it end?

Sometimes she just wants this, all of this, everything, to be over, but then she thinks she can't bear to lose a moment of it. He has awakened so many new parts of her and she lives, it seems, in a new state of craving. She craves his fingers, his tongue – she craves it, she craves all of it, she craves him. She has never thought, before, of her body as something they could both take pleasure in; and they do, together, minutely, until she comes, again and again, with a ferocity, thinking of it afterwards, that startles her. It is strange, she thinks, to think of all the people down the years who have discovered such pleasures, and all those who never have, or will. Strange to think that she, in almost any other set of circumstances, would have been one of those latter.

Sometimes she wonders . . . if her own mother – or Henry's – those bastions of her world – if one of them were to say to her, this happens once in a lifetime if you're fortunate, and life is so precarious these days, the sin would rather be *not* to do it. If they said that, if what they were to say was the opposite of what she knows they would, of what she knows is true: what difference, then, would it make?

Henry, returning home shortly after her, and heading straight for the decanter of brandy, pouring a large one and almost downing it, immediately pouring another, as he's begun to. Does he know? she thinks. Does he somehow sense it in her? She feels the weight of her responsibility to him, the gravitational pull, and she feels that particular, complicated ache for him, for all the ways they are bound together. For the births of their children, when he held her hand as the doctor placed the mask over her face and the sweet, faint creep of the chloroform began, and she felt herself spiralling backwards and under. For the cup of tea he insisted on bringing himself, hands shaking, when she came round each time. For the death of her father, when he carried the coffin, and held her as she sobbed. For the ways his fingers have tried to pleasure her.

She lays her head on his shoulder in bed and she listens as he talks, his hours upon hours spent logging ludicrous schemes by second-rate writers about how to defeat the enemy. Implausible stuff, impossible stuff. Dead bodies planted behind enemy lines with fake papers, fake ciphers, fake plans. Rumours seeded of stigmata and bleeding-eyed statues in Latin America, apparitions of the Virgin Mary and other doleful saints, to swing the superstitious their way. She presses her body closer to him and matches her breathing to his and strokes his stomach. In an odd way she loves Henry more than she ever has done, despite feeling further from him than she's ever been.

Nothing matters, insists Robert, when you might all die tomorrow, when you might all die tonight. But at the same time things must still matter somehow: they must, they do. It is impossible, whichever way you turn. *How does it end?* But of course it ends in death: everything does, and likely sooner than later, these London days. Whichever way she looks, there is no way out. She's a coward, she knows: just waiting to see what happens next. Because where, where could the place that they'd go, where could it possibly be?

Robert, meanwhile, on his portable typewriter as soon as she goes, until the very last minute before he has to report for duty. *Lived with long and dreamily*, he finally types, and he tugs out the page and holds it, reads it through once more, then signs it, hand trembling a little, *to Constance with love*, before folding it up and slipping it into his inner pocket, in case he does die tonight, an alternative ending.

Towards the end, they spend one night together: one whole night, and morning. It is reckless, Constance knows. Henry may have telephoned her sector post to find she was not on duty after all and so she will have to make up a story, something suitably alarming, the rush to a public air raid shelter, its metal bunks and warm and foetid air, and he will have been worried beyond belief, and it is unconscionable, and scares her, the hard, cold, unfamiliar part of her that is able, that is willing, to do this.

But the night has been theirs, and they have woken to the morning in each other's arms, skin against skin, hearts beating.

That late-spring early morning, blackout blind raised, they watch a dogfight in the sky, almost directly overhead. There hasn't been a mass raid in daylight for months, though sometimes at dawn you see the German planes returning. But today, through the copper-orange sky, they watch as a raiding party, half a dozen of them, is met by defending fighters, dived upon and side-slipping away and swooping back, arching and curling, gliding, before two spiral down in slow motion, sycamore seeds darkly falling, and the others somehow vanish, leaving white trails fading. It lasts a few seconds at most, but as they stand there it feels a lifetime, a desolate ballet choreographed only for them.

The two of them before the window.

For a while longer, neither of them moves.

Constance has spent the whole night trying to find the words to formulate a question that isn't even a question, a question she couldn't ask him even if she did find them.

I miss you, she thinks, and she does. She misses him the way you miss your children, the previous incarnations of them, even as you hold them, even as you hold and cherish and laugh and are proud of each new stage, each milestone, each person they become. She misses their childhood together, she misses their future . . . She even, she thinks, preposterously, misses him, the two of them, *now*; even now, as they stand by each other, she misses them.

I still sometimes wonder if one could draw a window in the wall, or in the air, and step through it together. This is what Constance says to Robert, in her mind. *To somewhere else, entirely new.*

There are gods and goddesses, he says to her in his mind, that he's been reading about, to whom you can take such a thing: whom you can implore, and who might even listen; whose impossible price might somehow be found. If only you knew where to find them, or to find the words that would unlock their portals, these guardians of unlived lives—

She turns to him then, as if she really has heard him.

Tell me where, she says silently, tell me how . . . her lovely face (he thinks) so open and beseeching, and he wishes, wishes, would give anything—

And now the moment's come: here it is: here they are, we are, now, and there is something they need from me, us, that is in our power to give them. Mine to give, perhaps, and yours to – bear witness?

So for a moment, look: I'm letting her see it. A sudden vision of her Robert at sixty, or seventy, so many long and happy years from now, a grandfather, capering round with grandchildren on a Richmond lawn that slopes to the river, romping and shrieking, still loose-limbed and gangly as a boy, as the man she knows.

Feel her bewilderment, feel her bewildered rising joy. It's cruel, it's too cruel to give this to her, I know, this thing that will never be, except in this brief moment she imagines it. But what else can I do? And wouldn't you?

If you could, Robert says, and he turns his back to the window and puts his arms around her one last time, left hand on the small of her back, pressing her close, right hand cupping the back of her head, fingers twining in her hair, would you do it, my love, would you know and change your fate?

Know your fate or change your fate?

Either. Both.

Wouldn't everyone?

No, he says. I think hardly anyone would.

I wonder if to know it is to inevitably want to change it. I wonder if that's why we never *can* know.

So would you?

Henry, she thinks. The boys in Hampshire. The close-trimmed yew and the close-kept lawn. Nasturtiums and the bed of dahlias restored. Tea with milk and sugar once again, and bacon and eggs on the silver breakfast platter, and seedcake made with butter. Sunday cricket matches on the village green, the young men returned, those who are going to, and the new bronze plaque with the names of those who won't buffed daily above fresh-cut lilies in the church. We made it through, we'll say, and everything is as it ought to be once more. How lucky, how lucky we are.

Unter den Linden

I COULD STILL REMEMBER THE VERB TABLES: the way the
feminine was also the plural, or the masculine the feminine,
or the masculine the plural, everything dependent, mutable.
We'd recited them at the start of every lesson, and I could
remember, too, the classroom we'd learned German in: the
laminate-topped desks, scored with graffiti from bored
compasses, the beige cast-iron radiators. And since I'd been
here I'd been thinking, also, of the small and terrible thing
that had happened in that room.

Der die das die, den die das die, dem der dem den.

I'd been to Germany twice before – once to visit a
penpal in Heidelberg, the second time on a school trip to
Aachen – but never to Berlin. I was in the city now for a
literature festival, several days of readings and workshops
and drinks receptions and discussions, and this was our
afternoon off. On the first morning there, we'd woken to
the news that Russia had launched a 'special military
operation' in Ukraine. It was unfathomable. Restless,
unable to rest, three of us had walked from our hotel in
Alexanderplatz, old East Berlin, towards the Brandenburg

Gate, a meandering route past museums and under railway arches, crossing then crossing again the Spree. It was that time of the day when the light can suddenly stream liquid, pink and gold and butterscotch, seeming to illuminate – the most austere of buildings, faces – almost from inside. The time of day between things.

Random German phrases had been rising, untethered, in my mind since we got here. *Der Bahnhof, das Wetter. Wie komme ich am besten zur Haltestelle, bitte? Gehen Sie geradeaus.* Gerrader-ise, we'd say, in our flat, self-conscious accents, the teacher trying to encourage us to do the proper throaty sounds, though any of our ostensible attempts at them were only ever done to make the others laugh. I remembered practising an accent inside my head that I'd never dare use.

We were talking as we walked, about everything, and nothing. Sure we were all living in a hallucination anyway, one of us said. None of this was real. It was just the product of what we expected to see. But the tanks, the bombs, the incendiaries: what fathomless horrors of what minds, or Mind, could or would create all this, and was it a surfeit of imagination, or a lack of it? And to what end this mutually assured deception?

In either case, we agreed, it was why the large windows of our hotel rooms, nine, thirteen, eighteen floors up, at 4 a.m. were so appealing. You twisted and yanked the handle to open them inwards and stepped forward to a thin glass balustrade, sharp and cold on the palms, and barely hipbone-height, far too low. The blank face of the opposite wall, the plummeting courtyard below: it was a too-easy cheat code, a reset, Game Over.

None of us said anything then, for a while. What was there to say? *Der die das die, den die das die, dem der dem den.* After school, in those days, after my homework was done, vocabulary memorised, declension of verbs complete, I used to boot up our BBC Micro, its curved screen that would jump with static and its red-and-black keyboard, beige metallic case, and play *SimCity*. I'd turn off the natural disasters mode, though more for me than them: what was the point of slowly, meticulously cultivating something if it could just be imperilled at any moment by the algorithm, earthquakes, volcanoes or meteor showers, fires breaking out, wrecking your budget and your careful build? There were disasters you couldn't turn off, like riots, or toxic spills, but they only happened if citizens were extremely unhappy with the state of their city, if transport and services were practically non-existent, and you always got warnings of that in their bulletins to you.

If you played the game long enough, the Sims were meant to progress to living in skyscrapers, great domes in the air, flying cars, though I never got far enough to see it. I always wondered, though: what then? Would they all decide, after that, to go back to nature, communes by the sea? They couldn't: they were in your hands. There was no end coded into the game, except to allow the impulse to burn it all down, to raze it to smouldering ruins, to nothing, in order that you could begin again.

To simulate: simulate what?

As we approached the Brandenburg Gate, a young man stopped so I could take a photograph of his sign, *FUCK PUTIN*, raising it higher, as high as he could. Another young man beside him, draped in the Ukrainian flag, with a sign saying *680km → Freiburg, 670km → Front*. A girl beside him, pink puffer coat and beanie, holding a piece of cardboard saying, *Wollen wir* something *bis es uns trifft?* The crucial verb covered over by her mitten, but the meaning, even with my decades-old German, was clear. Do we just wait until it's our turn?

What else were you supposed to do?

I thought of the anti-war march for Iraq: that had done fuck all, despite the feeling in the air that day that it had to, that it couldn't not matter. That was twenty years ago next year, I worked out, to the month. Twenty years: I felt dizzy. I'd barely been twenty myself then. I turned to look at the young people, marching on. They would change their world: they were sure of it. I thought how I'd read some-where that déjà vu was the closest thing we have to time travel; a chance to revisit, or at least reapprehend, and so to correct an experience. It had seemed pretty whimsical at the time. But now I thought of something we'd discussed as we walked, something Sontag said, about time existing so everything doesn't happen at once; space so that it doesn't happen just to you . . .

For the day that was in it, for a moment, then, standing there on Unter den Linden, I tried to think myself back: down past twenty, and that march; back down the other coordinates of my teenage years, to fourteen, thirteen, and that German classroom.

It was a small thing, in the grand scheme of things. One April Fool's Day we'd filled the teacher's spongy seat with water from our bottles, so that when she sat down her skirt would get wet. We'd filled it till it was completely saturated, couldn't hold another drop. Then we'd wiped down the legs and the floor with our scarves. She came in as usual, Guten Morgen, sat down. Her skirts were always thick tweed, so it would take a while for it to register. We recited our verb tables, not daring to make any eye contact with each other; watched her face. After a minute or so she shifted, then shifted again, lifted her haunches and then stood up, side-stepped to the nearest radiator, but we'd thought of that too, and cranked it to the right, tight, so it would be stone-cold.

We had been ready to deny it, to blame it on the previous class, to admit it, to blame each other, to gulder out, April Fool's! If she had only shouted at us, told us off, exclaimed, said something, anything, it would have been alright. Instead she said nothing, nothing. Instead, she went through the motions of teaching the rest of the class, her face blank and stricken.

If I could forget the memory of her face then I would.

She was a nervy teacher at the best of times, shy and easily flustered, too easy a target. When she began at our school at the start of that year, she'd had a framed picture of her two children on her desk, school uniforms and slightly buck teeth and sticky-out ears, until one day the picture had gone – nothing to do with us that time, but a prank played by another class, or maybe someone had made some innocently cruel remark, and she'd taken it down to protect herself, or them.

Those children, I thought, must have been the age of my own children now. I'd cried after FaceTiming them that morning, seeing them piled into my bed like puppies, squirming and jostling to kiss the phone. Why had I cried? Because they felt so far away, because it seemed impossible I'd ever get back to them. Because when I did, I knew I'd get exasperated with them, or cross, within minutes, even though they were all that mattered. Because I wasn't good enough for them. Because of this world, and the things people did to each other, and all the things I'd done, or failed to do.

After the lesson finished, that April Fool's, we knew we were in big trouble. That the teacher hadn't reacted straight away seemed proof of how serious it really was. Maybe we had half-thought it was a joke, or been able to kid ourselves that it could be: now we knew that it hadn't been. It had been something much meaner, crueller, that we had unleashed in ourselves. We braced ourselves all day: each time there was a knock on the door, it would be the vice principal, come to call us into her office one by one. Would we get away with just detention, or would they take it more seriously than that? The German teacher would have a fair idea who the ringleaders had been. We started almost wanting it to happen, just to get it over with. Several of us, several times, threatened to go to the staff room and confess, held back only by the threat of being called a tout.

But nothing did happen: not that day, or the next, or the next time we had a German lesson. Had the teacher dismissed it, after all, as a silly joke? Or had she not wanted to admit to her colleagues what had happened? Had she found a radiator in the corridor at breaktime, and sat on it till the tell-tale dark patch faded, and just endured the discomfort of the damp all day, the dull feeling of humiliation, and had she gone home to her children and cried, or snapped at them for something that wasn't their fault?

At the time, we told each other that we'd got away with it, but we hadn't, not at all.

I tried to stay with my own shame: to not push it away, but to breathe through it, let it go. If only you knew how – how to send an obliterating surge of love; how to dissolve the skeins of something that had already happened, that could not unhappen. I tried to breathe and look upwards, up at the sky. Lately I'd been trying to live, in theory if not much in practice, as if each moment might contain within it all that you needed to experience in that moment, be it boredom, or rage, or longing, or even something like an inexplicable joy. As if each soul was born exactly where it needed to be to dissolve the stagnation, the blockages, the despair, that only it so particularly could – until all dreary, tangling, entrapping stories were vanished, and peace could abound and we could be free.

To forgive yourself: for each tiny thing, for everything. To think that if each of us, every day, released a little more the pain of a past conflict, hurt, a betrayal, if each of us committed to doing what little we could to have peace, more peace, in our family, relationships, community, hearts, that these small acts, done consistently, and most of all done truly, could contribute to an entire paradigm shift. It was magical thinking. But for a moment, it almost seemed possible.

The light, in any case, was going now. We turned to walk back, each of us, who knows, fighting our own impossible battles, keeping our own impossible balance. A girl leapt into the arms of her teenage boyfriend: he swung her around, she shrieked with laughter. The setting sun caught the top of the Fernsehturm, the TV tower on

Alexanderplatz, and the cross on the top flashed gold. Then it too was gone, and the evening, for the lack of it, seemed to turn resolutely, bitterly cold. A fire engine barrelled past us, and another, yammering alarms. It came back, in a sickening jolt, all that was happening in the world, all that was happening just six hundred kilometres away, all that this night would and might bring. When people say, it's unimaginable, often what they mean is that they'd rather not. Nothing is unimaginable, except maybe what hasn't happened yet, as if by virtue of willpower we could make a different future for ourselves.

The lime trees along the whole length of the road that took their name were grave and withdrawn, silhouettes, their limbs against the sky infinitely augmenting diminishing fractals of themselves. There weren't yet any signs of spring, none at all.

Cuddies

MY GODMOTHER TOOK ME ASIDE on the morning I got married, and told me to remember always to put my husband first. She knew it sounded old-fashioned, she said, but I should never refuse him sex if he initiated it – should never let that side of things slide. I thought she was joking: looked around for my uni friends to burst out from where they must be in cahoots, but she was serious.

She was a serious sort of person – a music teacher, and a violinist in the local orchestra. There was always something hypnotic about watching her, straight-backed in her long black dress, hair in a tight bun, her attention focused on the conductor and whatever slight movement he might make.

She looked at me that morning with the same sort of urgency – an earnest expectancy.

'Why?' I said. 'What about if I'm on my period, or don't feel like it? What about – *feminism*?'

'It is a conversation between you,' she said, 'that you must keep open.'

I wanted this conversation to be over.

'Ok,' I said. 'Sure. Thanks for the advice.'

She looked like she was about to say something more, but didn't.

That night, I laughed about it with my new husband until neither of us could breathe for laughing. We were good then. He was working for a new start-up, working all hours, but it was something that he really believed in, connecting music fans with live gigs. I had just won a small award and a residency for the translation of a novella by a young German poet. Everything was ahead of us. For the first couple of years of our married life, it was trips to Berlin, conversations about literature in underground bars in Kreuzberg, performance art pieces where people stripped naked and threw themselves into the Wannsee. It was trips to San Francisco, and once to LA, the sunshine, the freeway, a weekend in someone's white clapboard house on the beach in Malibu. We burned through it, that bit of our lives, spending it freely, recklessly.

And then we had kids.

My husband had wanted children as much as I did, in theory. But he'd only reluctantly agreed to a third – and was adamant that we wouldn't, couldn't possibly, have a fourth. He was impatient now for these baby years to be over: still thought, or hoped, that they were just us on pause, a sort of limbo, after which we'd pick up where we left off, without realising that, for me, that could only ever be a diminishment. My godmother had never had children. In a *Sophie's Choice*-style scenario, it would be them, no question.

It was in the knowledge of this that I agreed to go on Jessica's birthday weekend. She'd been one of my closest friends at uni, but our lives were very different now. She worked in TV production, pretty high up these days, and had never wanted children; we had, maybe inevitably, drifted apart. But for her fortieth, she was hiring an oast house in the Sussex countryside, and wanted, as she put it, to get the Manchester gang back together. The photos in the link she emailed did look stunning – the oldest parts of the house were sixteenth-century, Grade II-listed and recently renovated with no expense spared, brick roundels with their distinctive white kilns that had once dried hops, master bedrooms inside the roundels with four-poster beds and roll-top baths, a further suite of bedrooms in a converted stable block. The oast house had beautiful gardens, its own little lake with a weeping willow tree, an outdoor hot tub, and it came with a wine-tasting tour of a neighbouring vineyard, and a private chef.

Despite all of this, I didn't want to go. I was yet to leave the girls for a night – was still breastfeeding my youngest. But my husband insisted that I needed a break. He said it would be good for me, to reconnect with old friends, drink wine, lie in till whatever time I wanted. What he didn't say, but I knew he meant, was that my life was far too wrapped up in the children – too bound up by them. He didn't approve, though he'd never have said this directly either, of my still breastfeeding an eighteen-month-old. He said, for God's sake, it was only a forty-five-minute drive from us in Brighton – I could be home in little more than a heartbeat if I was needed. He even offered to enlist my mother to fly over for the weekend to help look after the girls if I didn't trust him to cope. It was the closest we'd come to having a proper argument – not just bickering, tired squabbles or passive-aggressive needling, but the sort of argument that can open like a trapdoor beneath you, taking you, taking everything, with it. I emailed Jecca to say I'd be there.

And it was, yes, in a lot of ways very lovely. It was mid-June, almost the solstice, that moment when the sun is stilled in the sky, when there is technically no night, just overlapping waves of dusk into dawn into dusk. That first night, we ate good food, drank champagne, sat out on the decked terrace or in the hot tub, talking, smoking some weed that someone had brought. There were fourteen of us in total, a few of whom I knew, some from way back, some I didn't, two couples, a couple of mothers who, like me, had left the children alone with their father – not babysitting, they said, because a parent by definition couldn't: and nobody ever said of a mother that she was 'babysitting' her own children. There were some TV colleagues of Jecca's, an actress who'd been nominated for a BAFTA in something Jecca had produced, an actor who'd also been at university with us, though had always been more her friend than mine, had been famous then in our year for his peroxide hair and his bisexuality. He was from Northern Ireland too, and so we'd circled each other a bit uneasily, never quite become friends – he'd known that I knew, I always felt, that the hair, the flagrant sexuality, were likely something he'd acquired on the Stena Line, and would be toned down, a beanie put on, the eyeliner taken off, on the way back over.

On the second day we had the tour of the vineyard, drank more wine over lunch and got into an intense discussion about some friends of Jecca's who'd recently broken up. No one else knew them, so it was easy to discuss them in the abstract. They weren't married, had no children, but they'd been together twenty years. They'd decided to get out of the rat race of London, had bought a house in the country, but on the very night they moved into it, decided that it was over. There was nobody else, on either side, so far as Jecca knew. They had simply both decided, in that moment, No. No to the country house, to the dream, to all that might be expected to follow – a baby, or a dog – and, by extension, to each other.

Jecca told the story with a sort of zeal – with admiration. She thought the decision had a real bravery, a purity to it. But others were more circumspect. You wanted to ask the couple, people said, do you really think it gets better than this? You've known each other half your lives – you've had the best of each other. You've been through, let's say, the deaths of parents, or job losses, or depression, or whatever – who by forty hasn't? You've accommodated yourself to each other, worked out how to be – in bed, at family occasions, at dinner parties, on holiday. On hungover mornings together, or Sunday afternoons, or Januaries. The value of all of that incremental knowledge of someone, the cost of it – it isn't nothing. You can't just ditch it in one mad night. And besides, what else was it they were hoping for? The same again, with someone else?

A single life, one man pronounced solemnly, was never going to be the same in your forties as your twenties, or even your thirties.

'Fuck you!' Jecca said, and chucked the dregs of her glass of wine, only half-jokingly, in his direction.

Someone else suggested that maybe the chance that it *might* get better was enough. Maybe it was a relief to think of being with someone who knew nothing of the rest of you.

Would that really be liberation, another chipped in, or a sort of loneliness?

'For fuck's sake,' said the man who'd had the wine chucked at him, 'I'm forty-five. My hair is grey. My back is fucked. If I meet someone now, this is as good as I get. But my partner looks at me and sees, yes, obviously this, but also how I was when I was thirty and fit,' and his partner said, 'Dream on, babe', and everyone laughed, and the discussion became about mid-life crises, and what was a mid-life crisis, and how for men it was easier because if you chucked your life up in the air you could just start again, only why would you *want* to do the whole same thing, if it hadn't brought happiness the first time, and what about the children, if you had them . . . and on it went.

I didn't contribute much. I had drunk too much on the wine tour, and I was tired – away from the girls, far from luxuriating in a lie-in, I'd barely slept at all. My room was in one of the roundels, where the kiln used to be, and it was hot and airless, and the four-poster bed had creaked with every movement. The noise of the pipes, the sound of other people's footsteps, a pair of owls swooping back and forth and calling outside – my body had worked itself into a state of hyper-alertness. I convinced myself I could sense my toddler's night-waking. She was inconsolable, needing me and only me, unable to accept or to understand that I wasn't there. My eldest daughter was having one of the nightmares that had racked her lately, I was convinced of that too, and my middle one had woken when her older sister did and was starting up with her questions about death, and you had to answer her so carefully, and if my husband gave the wrong answer—

My mind went round and round, consuming itself. The other mums at the oast house had joked about how nice it was to go to the loo by yourself for a change, about how toddlers mauled your body, and even older children treated it as if it was an extension of theirs, no respect, no privacy. But without the girls, at least two out of three of whom ended up in my bed on any given night, I just felt unmoored.

'What about you?' someone said. It was the Nordie actor, sitting across the table from me. 'You haven't said. What would you do differently?'

'What would I do differently?' I repeated, a bit inanely.

'If you started your life again – from this moment – now.'

'I don't know,' I said. 'Nothing, I don't think.'

'You wouldn't change anything, so you wouldn't,' he said mockingly. 'Not a single thing.'

I thought of bare rooms with discoloured squares of wallpaper, of pockmarks in the carpets where the feet of furniture had been.

'I don't think so,' I said.

'Ach, wise up. Not a *single thing.*'

'Leave her alone, Marty,' someone said, and he just laughed.

Later, everyone swam in the lake. A handful, led by Jecca, skinny-dipped, and a couple of women compromised and went topless. I had only brought one costume with me, the functional black Speedo that I used for baby swimming classes, wormy with frayed elastic threads and saggy at the bottom. It was more embarrassing to insist on wearing that, and so look prudish, than to go completely naked, but as I took off my clothes I felt miserably self-conscious of my lopsided breasts and my belly with its livid Caesarean scars, the purple stretch marks and spatters of burst veins on my thighs, my unshaven legs, my completely neglected scroag of pubic hair. I thought of the ways my godmother and my mum would talk of other women: 'Did you see the state of her?' 'She's let herself go', 'Sure she's nothing but a slut', and the times in my teenage years I'd get so cross at them, and say that, anyway, *slut* meant something entirely different, though just as pejorative, these days.

Of course there were things I would change, I said angrily to Marty in my head, as I watched him with the naked BAFTA-nominated actress on his shoulders, steadying her feet in his hands as she raised herself up and somersaulted over him into the water. But what would the price of them be? And then I thought, No – I'm proud, proud of these scars, proud of the way my body tells the stories of the gestations of my girls, proud of the ways it makes sense when I'm with them. For them, I was home – I was the warm, soft body that fed them, that held them, picked them up, pillowed them, cuddled them. They didn't see me any other way: or rather, they did, they just saw *me*, though I supposed they'd look at me differently – critically, disdainfully, maybe even disgust-edly – one day.

I tried to push away the thought. I thought instead of telling my husband later that I'd been skinny-dipping, and how he'd think of the Wannsee, of how we'd giggled like crazy when the performance artists started stripping off and hurling themselves in, hollering at the audience to join them, and then how we'd thought, screw it, and joined them. He'd like that I was doing this.

The water, as I edged my way in, was cool and green and murky, and the bottom of the lake, which turned out to be quite shallow, was a sludge of mud and decomposing leaves which sucked in your ankles. But I could tell it in a wild and romantic way, I thought, when I told him – I could try to make it sound sexy.

That evening, Marty handed round MDMA pills. They were bright blue and had *SKY* stamped on them. I held mine in the palm of my hand, already knowing I wasn't going to take it.

'It's good stuff,' he said, 'promise.'

Then he said, 'You're not going to take it, are you?'

'No,' I said.

'Why not?'

'I just don't want to.'

'Jecca thinks you're not having a good time.'

'I'm having a great time,' I said.

He smiled. 'Sure, I forgot. Your life is perfect. It's the rest of us fuck-ups who need all the help we can get.' He took the pill back from my palm, delicately, mockingly, finger and thumb, little finger out like he was miming drinking a posh cup of tea, and put it on his own tongue. I was suddenly raging with him.

'Of course it isn't perfect,' I said.

And of course it wasn't. My husband did damage limitation for one of the biggest social media conglomerates, and I had the dull but regular work of checking the rendering of technical manuals for home appliances into English – not exactly what you dreamed of. But mainly, it was that we didn't have sex any more. He'd been squeamish about sex while I was pregnant – at the start, when it felt so strange and new and fragile, and later, when I had a bump, and a baby visibly moving inside – even when I was overdue, and the midwife told us we should have sex to try to get things moving. By the time our firstborn was a few months old, we'd found ways of having sex again – and if it wasn't like we used to, still there was something exciting in the urgency of it, against the kitchen countertop or on the sofa, or with the baby in the buggy in the hall. But as soon as I was pregnant with our second, the same thing had happened, his reluctance. That had been a difficult birth, back to back, shoulder dystocia, ending in an emergency Caesarean. The recovery time was much longer, the logistics, with two under two, were far more difficult, and she didn't take a bottle easily – he didn't think it felt right to have sex while I was still breastfeeding. Our third had been conceived drunkenly on our anniversary – and that was the last time we'd had proper sex. We'd touched each other a bit, occasionally, but I couldn't remember the last time we'd properly kissed, even.

I felt my eyes, stupidly, flood with tears.

'Oh God,' he said. 'Ach, here, I'm sorry. I didn't mean to—'

'Don't worry about it,' I said. 'I'm just tired. The wains,' I said. 'I'm not used to leaving them. I didn't sleep.'

'I've Xanax,' he said. 'Sure let me give you a Xanax for tonight. That will help.'

'Ok,' I said. 'Whatever, maybe. Look, I'm sorry, I feel so scundered.' I was still crying stupid tears.

'Don't be scundered. You used to be, like, Jecca's ice maiden friend.'

'*Ice* maiden?'

'Like you always dressed in black, so you did, and you were studying French and Russian—'

'German and Russian. Though I can't believe you remember that.'

'—and we had this conversation once about the existentialists. You told me to read de Beauvoir. How to live at the crossroads of freedom and facticity.'

'I don't remember that.' There was so much that I didn't even realise I'd forgotten. I didn't even really remember what *facticity* meant. 'I can't believe you thought I was an ice maiden. I honestly wasn't. I think I was just shy. All those English girls. Jeccas and Beccas and Lozzas and Chezzas – I mainly felt like a great big culchie.'

He laughed. 'Coming from a denizen of the metropolis of Belfast, that's saying something. Try being a wee lad from a farm in Fermanagh.'

'Do you get back much?' I said.

'Nope. You?'

'Not really. I try to get back for the girls to see my folks, but three under five's not easy.'

He whistled. 'Three wee cuddies.'

Now I laughed. 'I don't think I've heard that word in years.'

We looked at each other. He smiled, wryly, and I felt his smile mirror itself on my face. There was no one else here who would have understood what he meant. I felt suddenly tired. Jecca was forty – we were all turning forty – how had that happened? I wanted another baby, or at least I thought I did, or maybe it was that I didn't want this stage of life to end – or the next one to start. Whatever it might be.

'Look,' he said. His pupils were going big and glassy – he

must have taken a first dose already, he was starting to come up. 'Take care of yourself, won't you?'

By midnight, I was well and truly done in – I decided to leave the rest of them to it. Not everyone was high, but it was becoming boring not to be. I lay in bed for a while, but even with earplugs in I couldn't sleep – the house's sound system was too good, and my bedroom was right above it. Midnight turned to one a.m., two. Three a.m. I heard voices in the corridor, Jecca, and a couple of others – and Marty. I got up, went to my door, opened it.

'Marty,' I said.

The four of them were hugging, laughing, didn't hear me. I could barely hear myself, suddenly, over the thudding of my heart. I called a bit louder. 'Here, Marty?'

He turned round.

'Sian? That you?'

I realised I was just in my t-shirt and pants. The corridor was dark, but I closed the door over a bit.

'Could I've that Xanax?' I said.

'Ya wee hallion,' he said. 'Sure, no probs, I'll get it right away.'

I shut the door and stood for a moment. Then I pulled off the old t-shirt and put on the dress I'd been wearing earlier, for modesty's sake, because I didn't want it to look like I was seducing him. Only of course he wouldn't think that, would he? Because I wasn't, was I?

Almost no time had passed before he was tapping on the door. I opened it and he came in, and we looked at each other, and then he was kissing me. He'd barely touched me when the milk released, like relief turned liquid. I felt the patches spread, quickly, easily through the thin cotton of my dress. I pulled away from him.

'You don't want to do this?' he said.

'It's not that.'

I touched my chest – his fingers followed. I was only breastfeeding at night, but maybe more than I'd realised, because my breasts had swelled up badly on the first night, that tight, pressing ache – lopsided, because the left was the side my toddler slept on when she climbed into my bed, and so that was the side I always lazily let her suckle from. He felt inside the neckline of my dress, then started to lift it over my head – I let him. He pushed me gently to the bed – put his mouth to my nipple, softly, then harder.

'That doesn't hurt, does it?' he said. I laughed. He had no idea how tight the latch of a baby was – or the feeling of a toddler's eager, inadvertent teeth.

'What?' he said.

'It doesn't hurt.'

'It's so sweet,' he said, and licked the sheen of milk from my breast, from its underside, from where it had pooled slightly in the hollow at the base of my ribcage, and it was so unexpected, so intimate an act, that a new dimension seemed to open up inside of me – that's the best way of putting it that I have, some new capacity to hunger and be sated and to hunger. And I felt him feel it – whatever animal instincts he had that were attuned to sex.

'What would you like me to do?' he said. But even as he asked he was moving my limbs, turning me over, positioning me, and what I wanted was just to give myself over, pure physical sensation, the abandon of it. And I suppose that something of a sort of, for want of a better word, pride, kicked in as well: I hadn't slept with very many people at all, I knew he had, women and men, and I was suddenly determined that he not be acting out of some sense of pity, that he be satisfied, too, by more than whatever the novelty of this experience might be for him.

'Whatever you want,' I said. 'Everything.'

It was fully light outside by the time he left. Some of the others were up and swimming in the lake again already. I lay there feeling real in a physical sense, but otherwise entirely unreal. I tried to imagine arriving back home – walking through the door, just a few hours from now, just a few miles away. I couldn't. Then, to my surprise, even without the Xanax, I slept deeply. When I woke, it was past noon, and the flurry of departures had begun. He had already gone – there were rail strikes, and someone had offered a lift back to London. He had emailed to say as much – he must have found my email on the round-robin list. His email ended with *Let me know if you'd like to grab a drink sometime*, and his mobile number, and *xx*. But it was a generic email, generically polite, and I knew I wouldn't reply. What was there to say? I wasn't going to get my husband to take a day off work so I could go gallivanting up to London, and nor was he going to take a train down to the sea for the day to walk around from playground to playground while I pushed a buggy my toddler refused to sit in, until it was time for nursery pick-up and the school run. I didn't want an affair. Those bare rooms with discoloured paper, pockmarked carpets. I didn't want that. I didn't want anything different – I did want what I had, I really did. I wanted all of it, I thought, as fully as I could, as fully as I could possibly have it.

It was a relief to get home. It was a relief to realise, too, that I didn't feel anything resembling guilt. I couldn't think of a single story where the adulterous woman wasn't punished – not a single one. But where guilt should have been, I felt instead a sort of satiety, and that new awareness of hunger. I would start seducing my husband again, I thought, and I thought that my godmother had been right, in a way, after all: it was the thing that had fundamentally changed, that the central channels of my intimacy were no longer directed at him. That is what she'd meant, I thought: that you had to keep them clear, keep it running, keep it flowing between you. And of course it was impossible, but you had to try, and you had to try harder, and I would.

Daphne

THE GREAT MURMURATION OF STARLINGS had gone from East Belfast – just gone. She let one bus go by, then another, as she stood watching the sky. She hadn't believed it, when she heard them discussing it on the radio this morning. Sure, you looked up over the Albert Bridge on a winter's afternoon and saw hundreds of them, thousands, a swirling, shape-shifting mass, swooping first this way then abruptly that, up the river and right back down, spreading out across the whole sky then coming back into a tight dark ball, as the sky put on its own show of turning a dozen shades of pink and orange. But now – nothing.

The sky, her aunt Mary once told her, was nothing to do with shepherds or delight – it was that colour on account of pollution, all the particles of dust and debris and exhaust fumes trapped in the atmosphere. And it was down to light pollution too, that the starlings had gone – on the radio they said the extent of housing develop-ment along the Lagan and the new LED lights on the bridge were to blame, though your man from the Department said all lighting was compliant with current regulations and the RSPB lady said you needed to look at the whole picture, as we'd lost three-quarters of our starlings in the last thirty years.

It had made her desperately tired, hearing that. To think that her own grandchildren wouldn't stand there juking up till their necks were cricked asking, Who was the ringleader? Who said, Now turn? and wondering why they never crashed, because they never did, never, not one of them turned the wrong way or a moment too soon, like they were following some invisible pattern in the sky, giving themselves over to something that would be there for us too, if we could only see it.

She craned her own neck one last time. But the night had set in now and the river flowed round the bend and on, reflecting only vague shapes of clouds in its sodium lights. Oh Lagan, she thought impulsively, great god of the river, help us, won't you, help your wee creatures. She was immediately mortified at herself. Who did she think she was? She sighed and hefted her tote bag onto her shoulder.

There was a 4d bus approaching now, flat pink face nosing through the traffic. She turned her back fully on the river and shuffled into line.

She got the front seat of the top deck, which cheered her up, and arranged her messages carefully at her feet. Uppermost were two iced buns she'd hide away and give to her grandsons tomorrow. She'd started looking after one on Monday and Friday, and the other on Wednesday and Friday, to help out her daughters-in-law – both her sons had married English girls, both had convinced them to move back here; she'd no idea why, though she never said as much aloud. They'd had babies within a month of each other, but the similarities stopped there: one ate puréed food you zoomed into his mouth on an aeroplane, but you weren't allowed to do that to the other – he'd to feed himself, cut-up sticks and cubes and handfuls of things that he chose and discarded at will, and if he threw them down to the floor you weren't to react. One had to be put in the travel cot at exactly the same time each day for a precise number of minutes, was woken on the dot, and ignored if he woke before that, even if he cried. The other needed someone to lie down beside him, and wasn't to be let cry a minute.

Both daughters-in-law were unanimous on only one front: neither child was to have sugar.

But where was the fun in that? Wasn't being a granny all about spoiling the wains, so they'd cuddle up to you and love you, and not start gurning and guldering the moment they saw you? She'd scrub off every sticky trace from their gubs, and nobody'd be any the wiser. If they started babbling about iced buns, well, their mummies would think they'd got it off the TV, except the one that wasn't meant to watch any screens, only how else were you meant to entertain a pair of one-year-olds for the whole entire day? How had she done it?

Looking back, she didn't actually remember much of those years. The grind of it. The sleeplessness, the bickering.

The just getting on with it, getting by. It was why being a grandparent was supposed to be a joy – the chance to experience it as you wished it had been, in smaller doses. She'd imagined being a grandma would involve stirring up Christmas puddings, the wains on wee wooden stools with wee matching aprons beside you, taking it in turns to heave round the big wooden spoon. Though where she'd got the notion she hadn't a baldy, for her mother never bothered making a pudding when you could buy a perfectly decent one at the Co-op – and her own grandma hadn't been a pudding-mixing sort, not at all. Her grandma had had a face like a bulldog, and had mainly sat on her stool in the doorway, smoking her fegs and glowering at the street, not paying you any mind as you dared each other to sneak up beside her and touch the edge of her shawl, till she'd suddenly whip off her slipper and hurl it at you as you ran away like the clappers. In the whole of her childhood, the big ceramic basin was only ever used for the sick bowl, give or take the occasional batch of fairy-cakes.

Surely that couldn't be right, could it?

But she remembered the basin, the beige inside of it, the places where the blue outer paint was chipped, the weight of it in your lap as you miserably waited to puke. Scrubbed out and put back on its shelf. Oh, my days . . . There was definitely, she thought, reaching over to press the button for her stop, such a thing as rose-tinted spectacles. Starlings or not, you had to remember that.

But the starlings – or lack of them – had got her thinking. Her neat back garden, Astroturfed by one of her sons so it'd be less hassle for her – he'd been pleased at that, and she hadn't wanted to ask was it himself he was really sparing, pushing the rusty old lawnmower up and down each week. The birch-panelled fence, which her husband put up just before he died, to replace the unruly privet hedge – it always seemed to her full of eyes, ever-watching, a sort of CCTV that would put off any wee creature from venturing onto the lawn. They used to have hedgehogs before, when the boys were small, when the house was on the edge of the fields, before the estate spread further. You put out dog food for them, not bread soaked in milk, she remembered that. But when had she last seen a hedgehog? And how was a hedgehog to get through a vigilant fence?

Saturday, after a whole day of both toddlers, she was able for nothing. But on Sunday she took the bus up to the big garden centre at Dundonald. It dismayed her to see that even amidst the bird baths and toad dens, the bug hotels, bat boxes and nesting boxes, the labels celebrating plants good for pollinators, there was roll upon roll of fake grass and 'fauxliage', strings of plastic jasmine and ivy, and weed-killer, so much weed-killer. Oh, she knew they had to cater to their customers – they were a business, after all. But it would make you want to weep, the hours of your life you'd spent dripping poison onto patches of soft spongy moss, or yanking dandelions from the lawn, the pale crisp taproots and hairy tough leaves, when you now realised you should have been celebrating them – the brightness of their yellow, like wee sunbursts, the delicacy of their ghostly orbs. You should have been – oh – pulling the leaves for salad, or making tinctures with the roots, though she'd like to have seen Geoffrey's face if she'd given him a plate of dandelion from the garden, and she was only vague on what a tincture actually was. But even so!

She loaded her trolley with anything that looked good for wildlife. That was what the lady on the radio had said – start by tending to your own garden. At the till, she impulsively picked up a couple of wildflower seed-bombs for the wains to chuck around, and a packet of something called 'root-grow'. She was still studying the 'root-grow' when it was her turn to pay.

'Magic stuff,' said the girl at the till.

She confessed she'd never heard of it before.

It was mycorrhizal fungi, the girl said, and symbiosis, and a lot of other words she smiled and nodded at.

'Basically,' the girl said, taking pity on her, 'put it this way – it'll make anything grow bigger and better than it ever thought it could.'

She told the girl she'd take it.

Back home, she worked till her nails were ragged and her joints ached and her slacks were completely gone at the knee, ripping up the Astroturf and hacking holes in the fence, at first hedgehog-sized, then – feck it, she thought – big enough for foxes or maybe even badgers, if they were bould enough to shoulder their way through the splinters. Then she threw around the wild seed and the 'root-grow', imagining the meadow that would spring up. It would be up to her waist – thrumming with bees – a paradise. A wild satisfaction drove her on, and it wasn't till she was sitting by the back patio door, feet in the washing-up basin of hot water, that she realised how much of a hames the garden looked. The neighbours would be complaining to her sons, no doubt, but she'd tell them about the starlings, she'd say it wasn't just the starlings we were losing when we lost them, and they'd understand, she thought, surely they would?

And if the daughters-in-law were appalled at the mess and the muck, or the thought of their wee boys in it, at least the boys would love it, mud pies and digging for worms . . . She suddenly wished with her whole heart she'd let her own boys do more of that, instead of insisting they keep their clothes clean, giving them an earful if they came home with lichen smears on their trousers or blazer buttons gone from climbing trees. Oh! she missed them. She missed them like you must miss phantom limbs – with a pain that was greater than any physical pain could be. How did it just go, without your knowing? Dwindling, dwindling, till you didn't even think to notice it was gone.

'Daphne', her eldest had taken to calling her since his father died, as if he was the man of the family now, and her younger had copied him, as he always did. It was ironic, was that the word, or maybe she meant infantilising, a clumsy way of trying to show that they'd take care of her. Now everyone called her 'Daphne', even the wains had their own version of it. But she'd hated the name since she learned it just meant a woman in a myth who'd been turned to a tree. What sort of a story, her ten-year-old self had said in disgust, was that to be named for?

'I just thought it suited you,' her mother said, and her father said, 'Maybe you'll grow into it.'

She closed her eyes. Her poor feet throbbed, fit to burst. Before scattering it, she'd opened the packet of 'root-grow' to inspect it – had wet the tip of her finger and touched the powdery-white grains inside, on impulse touched it to her tongue. It was ridiculous, she knew, but she imagined now, just for a moment, that there actually were roots struggling to break through the soles of her feet, through each of her toes. Thin pale filaments – determined. Her fingers, too, so stiff and bleeding, were about to froth into bud at the tips, if only she'd let them. She could take herself to the middle of her woebegone lawn, and root down, through the choco-latey layers of earth, to where hidden streams ran, and at the same time she'd rise, straight-backed and twelve foot tall, thrumming with sweet sap, headily, intoxicatingly fragrant, and the meadow would leap to life and sway around her and starlings, magically restored, would flock and birl.

'Catch yourself on,' she said to herself, as sternly as she could. 'Sure they'd only shit all over you.'

Laughing aloud to herself, only a little bit frightened, she was already imagining tearing open a fresh packet of the magic stuff, stirring it into a cup of tea, and gulping it down.

Bibi

SPRING IN MARRAKECH: profusions of bougainvillea and the deep red of hibiscus flowers, long tongues quivering for their bees. The hum of those bees, and the chatter of sparrows, and the pulse of crickets. Peacocks in the olive groves, strutting and pecking, leaping to perch on branches and survey their domain. The pink clay paths of the kasbah, polished smooth and occasionally cracked by the sun; the spiky grass, the cypress trees. The morning's chill giving way already to a fiercening sun, bright light and sharp-edged shadows. The men already at work in the rose gardens, long loose shirts and wide-brimmed hats, the heave and thud of their long curved blades, the snow-capped Atlas Mountains behind them on the horizon. Bowls of those roses freshly cut and placed on the tables under the loose thatched canopy, yellow and orange and peach tinged with white, cream tinged with pink, ardent, extravagant blooms you'd need both hands to cup.

At this time of the morning, the waiters are setting up for breakfast service on the terrace, orange juice pressed from the kasbah's own oranges, silver pots of sweet mint tea, pots of coffee. Baskets of eggs to be made into omelettes, pancakes flipped on a hotplate and piled in earthenware dishes. Last night's bread split and toasted to go with pale cubes of butter and dark honey and a tangy, floral conserve made from loquats. A dish of green melon.

Cats slink between the table legs, hungry, impatient; their plucky kittens pounce at shadows, at sparrows, at scattered petals caught in a sudden breeze.

It is paradise here.

They have settled into the rhythm of the days, and only three, four, five days in, their normal lives seem far away. They wake later than usual, amble to breakfast, breakfast lazily. Afterwards they wander through the gardens, past the citrus and the pomegranate trees, to the lily pond with the tadpoles, to the other pond in the shade of the sprawling fig tree to watch the huge toads, olive-coloured with orange spots and pale beige bellies, clambering over and onto each other, surprisingly nimble for their size. They visit the donkeys, who come to the edge of their pen twitching their long furry ears in anticipation of the windfall oranges and figs that the girls like to give them, dashing forward to drop them over the wooden fence then retreating to watch the animals' velvety lips peeling up from square yellow teeth as they nibble and nuzzle at the fruit. Sometimes a donkey will throw back its head and neck and bray, such a ludicrous, rusty, ear-splitting noise. The younger two compete then to out-donkey each other, eee-ore, eee-*ore*, until their father, laughing, shushes them for the sake of the other guests.

After their stroll they go back and get ready to swim — there are two pools in the kasbah's estate, the bigger one open-air, the smaller one under a glass roof, and heated. They always start off in this one, because the older girls, who are kind, patient, protective of her, are teaching their youngest sister to swim. At the start of the holiday she was in armbands and a flotation suit: now she can manage to doggy-paddle almost a width without anything, before she gets so excited at her achievement she forgets to kick, and goes spluttering under again. By mid-morning it's hot enough for the main pool, and so they jump in there, race each other, play, get out shivering to sit in the sun and wait to be warm enough to brave it again. What else do they do? Not much, and yet the time never seems to drag. They read, they drink the sweet mint tea and eat the biscuits that are brought to them poolside. The older girls giggle in exaggerated poses for the selfies they send to their friends.

She catches other guests glancing at them sometimes, trying to work them out. A single father with four daughters? But no: although they're still careful, in front of his older girls, to not be explicit, too casual, in the way they touch each other, the holiday has relaxed them into letting a hand rest on a bare thigh, or on the small of a back, a holding of hands as they walk through the gardens, the rubbing of suntan lotion in a way that's not filial. And then she feels people doing the maths: is it possible, just, that they are her children; that she had the eldest when she was the eldest's age herself? But no, she is too careful with them to be their mother, and he is too careful with her for her to be his wife of so many years. They work it out then: this is the age-old story of a mid-life crisis and a younger woman, and they are satisfied with the frisson of scandal.

In the afternoons, after lunch, they go back to their rooms to nap. Monique and Léa in their own room, which has a private terrace with an outdoor bathtub which they are thrilled about; a room which is already a confection of tangled bikinis and hair straighteners and discarded tops and make-up, the sort of bedroom she always dreamed of having. Their own is a big room with an adjoining annexe separated from the main space by a hanging tapestry, in which Elodie sleeps in a single bed. He lies down with Elodie and sings to her until she falls asleep, then ducks back through the tapestry to get into the four-poster bed with her, its taut sheets, cast-iron frame.

He is assiduous with her, attentive to her pleasure, and under his hands and his tongue her body is responsive, comes alive. It was a revelation, sex with him. Two of her previous boyfriends, her own age, had tried to choke her during sex – not even, she suspects, because they actually wanted to; just because they thought they could, or that it was something they were supposed to want. A third boyfriend, despite the fact they were together for almost a year, and sometimes used to stay up all night talking, had never seemed to want physical intimacy at all.

They use condoms, though her menstrual tracker tells her it's not a dangerous time of the month. Only once do they leave it too long before he puts one on, and he pulls out suddenly and comes on her back. After he wipes her down, while he's in the bathroom, washing himself, she takes out her phone and checks the app again. It's far too near her period, the calendar says, for conception to be possible. But still she wonders: if her cycle was off this month, or the dates are wrong. If, if: what then? What would she do?

She has never particularly wanted children: or rather, they have seemed such an abstract and unlikely thing, so impossible to imagine into her life, that she hasn't given them much thought. When he asked her, as he did early on, what she felt about it, she just said she's never wanted babies. He doesn't want any more: a sixteen-year-old, a twelve-year-old, a six-year-old, he is over the baby years. If she decided she did want a baby, she would have to make the case for it now; she would have to be adamant, determined, sure: which seems immoral, given that it's little more than a hedging of the hereafter against a theoretical sense of loss.

When he comes back into bed he kisses, playfully, each of her nipples. 'Hey you.'

She laughs. 'Hey.'

'That was nice,' he says, lying back.

'That was really nice.'

She curls sideways into him, rests her head on his chest. Breathes in the smell of him, sweaty and warm, that musky tinge of recent sex. Feels his heart beating, still not quite quelled.

'Your heart,' she says. 'It's still going fast.' She taps out the rhythm of it until it's fully slowed. 'There.'

'Are you happy?' he asks.

'Yes,' she says. 'Yes, I am.'

'I'm so glad,' he says, and exhales. 'Je t'aime, you know.'

'Je t'aime too.'

After their nap they all swim again, or play padel, a sort of cross between tennis and squash, on the little terracotta court under the bougainvillea and the indignant sparrows. She is ok at padel, but it's him and Monique who captain the teams, both fiercely competitive, slamming the ball at each other, roaring and shrieking and punching the air with each point missed or gained. Most evenings they stay in the kasbah, a glass of rosé wine for him, sometimes a rare glass for her too, and a Coke for the girls in the gardens, as the shadows soften and blur and the grasses move and the cypress trees seem to draw up into themselves; then they dine in the kasbah's little courtyard restaurant, lit at ground level by lanterns, the flickering light casting intricate patterns onto the tiled floor through the perforated brass. One afternoon they go into central Marrakech, to Jemaa el-Fnaa, the big central square with the fast agitated music of the snake charmers and the leaping tumbling acrobats, the hustlers and the beggars, the henna ladies, the men who come up to you with hand-held rattle-drums, with wooden snakes, pushing them at you, with Barbary macaques on chains. It's Ramadan, and as the sun sets the muezzins begin their call to prayer, overlapping waves of it flooding the square, the men on plastic stools beside their spread carpets of trinkets and wares washing themselves with bottles of water, unrolling prayer mats and beginning their devotions. The girls watch, big-eyed, and she feels herself watching big-eyed too. It feels ancient: it feels holy. It feels as if there are other ways you could be living your life. The moon, just days from being full, rising over the minaret of the Koutoubia Mosque like a blessing, or a promise. They stand there under it close together, all holding hands, and she thinks: I will always know now that places like this exist.

That night, searching in his washbag for Calpol meltlets for Elodie, who has woken with the growing pains that have tormented her lately, she finds his wedding ring. It is twisted up in a square of toilet paper from which it has come loose. She takes it out, holds it. In the early days of their relationship he still wore the ring, and she used to ask often about his wife – to show, she supposes, that she cared, that she understood, that she was mature enough to handle all of this. But at some point, although she'd talk about his wife if he did, or if the girls brought her up, she stopped initiating conversations herself. At some point, too, he stopped wearing his wedding ring. She didn't notice when, exactly: he'd always take it off if he was on a long bike ride, or playing squash. But there must have been a day when he didn't put it back on, and she wonders now if that was intentional, a conscious decision on his part; and what might have prompted it. It doesn't seem particularly cere-monial, kept in loo roll inside a washbag. She wonders if he knows it's there, or if he put it hastily or absent-mindedly there for safekeeping and then forgot it. She wonders if she should tell him that she has found it.

Elodie is howling. She folds up the ring in the toilet paper, slips it back inside the mesh pouch. Her hands are trembling. She delves again through the washbag until she finds the foiled silver squares of Calpol.

The following afternoon, she leaves them by the pool and goes back to the room to call her mother. They usually speak most days, though recently she's been trying to leave it two or three days between phone calls. This has been one of the longest stretches they haven't spoken. It rings and rings, which could be a good or a bad sign. It could mean her mother's doing something, not just maudlin on the sofa or scrolling through her phone in bed. On the other hand, she could be too far gone to answer, dropping it, swiping at it ineffectually.

Her mother always used to wait till six o'clock to have

her first drink — it was wine in those days. You'd see her glancing at the clock from half past five, and she'd snap at you or seem not to hear if you asked her a question. Then one summer it became a gin and tonic at five, 'A sundowner, they call it,' her mother said, 'all of those ex-pat types', even though sunset in the North, in summer, wasn't until gone ten, past bedtime. Her mother had been annoyed at her when she pointed this out: 'It's just a saying,' she'd said. 'It just marks the end of the day.' For a while then she called it her 'aperitif' instead, and after that it became a glass of something with lunch, 'sure the French and Italians do', then a Buck's Fizz mid-morning, as if the orange juice, the cheery associations with brunch, with movies, the bubbles, somehow made it ok. Then from time to time, for no ostensible reason, the arcane rules would change, and it would be back to waiting till lunchtime, or five, or even right back to six o'clock, for a while.

It is four o'clock in Morocco, an hour later than at home. The phone rings and rings. She wanders round the bedroom, which is cool and dim with the shutters closed. She opens them — closes them over again. Straightens a ruckled corner of a rug with her toe. Runs a hand along the decorative carving of the wardrobe. The phone rings, rings. Eventually her mother answers.

'Hello?' her mother says, as if she doesn't know who's calling, and this, too, is either vodka or an attempt at a dig.

'Hi Mum,' she says, 'it's only me.'

'Trixie, hiya!' her mother says, extravagantly. 'So tell me this: is it paradise there, is it? Is it everything you hoped and dreamed of?' Her mother is slightly slurring her words. It's better than the stage where she carefully enunciates them. 'So how is Captain von Trapp?' her mother goes on, before she's had a chance to reply.

'Mummy,' she says.

'See that film?' her mother says. 'It was always the Baroness I liked. Now there's a class act. She was well out of it, if you ask me. All those singing rug-rats. But,' she says, 'it's your life, and I'll not say another word about it.'

There comes the click and the kiss of her mother lighting a cigarette – the sigh of her exhale. As if channelling the Baroness makes even a Lambert & Butler from a box with a picture of rotten lungs glamorous.

She sits on the bed, his side of it, draws her knees up to her chest. She wants to say, 'How are you, Mum, what have you been up to?' but in certain moods that question, even asked lightly, will seem to her mother too freighted.

'It is lovely here,' she says instead.

'Well, that's nice,' says her mother.

There is a short silence. She listens to her mother smoking.

'Here!' her mother says. 'To change the subject. I was thinking I might go to university. Get a degree.'

'Right,' she says. 'That's great, Mum.'

'Well, you could try to sound a wee bit happier for me.'

'I am.'

'Well, you don't sound it, is all I'm saying.'

'I said it was great.'

'No you didn't: you said "great", in that sort of a way. If

you'd meant it, you could have said, "Great! That's great, Mum, I'm really happy for you!"'

She leans back against the pillows, closes her eyes. 'Where are you thinking of going,' she says, 'and when, and to study what, and what are the course requirements, have you looked into that? And how much will it cost, and how will you pay?'

'Jesus Christ,' her mother says. 'I mean for crying out loud.'

She has no idea how her mother's finances work. She knows that her uncle James, her mother's younger brother, who is a lawyer in Dubai, sends her money from time to time, though she has no idea how much, or on what basis. They haven't seen him in years, but she shouldn't judge him, isn't judging him – she wouldn't have been able to go to university herself without his help.

'Here's me telling you there's something I'd like to do,' her mother goes on, 'something really positive, that could be good for me, and what do you want to do but crush it from the get-go.'

She says nothing.

'Like you always do,' says her mother. 'Just like you always do.'

'I'm sorry,' she says, her eyes still closed. 'I think it sounds potentially really interesting. I just think . . .'

'You just think what?'

'Well, for starters,' she says, trying to soften her voice, 'what were you thinking of studying?'

'English!' her mother says triumphantly.

'English?' She hasn't seen her mother read a book in years.

'I used to read all the time, you know. While I was cooking. At the school gates. You probably don't remember, but the other mums used to comment on that about me, the way I was always reading. So I just thought: why not? Why not go to university, and do it properly.'

'I was just thinking of that massage therapy course you did, and the hairdressing, and the catering college . . .'

'None of them were *me*. That was the problem. This is different. It's what I've always wanted to do. Do you really not remember, the way we were always up at the library? I used to take you there twice a week. Do you not remember?'

'I do remember that,' she says.

'Well, there you go.'

She sits up, opens her eyes. The sudden movement makes stars dance across her vision, vortexes whirling in the dark.

'I'm going to have to go,' she says. 'It's three pound a minute to call from here.'

'Jesus. Well, on you go then, back to your nannying. I hope your man realises what a good thing he's got going. I hope he's treating you well.'

'He is, Mum,' she says. And then she says, 'Here, Mummy—' but it's too late. Her mother is already saying, 'Bye-bye, bye-bye now, bye-bye' – and the phone has gone dead.

She doesn't even really know what she was going to say. She lies back again. The bedlinen smells of him – of them.

It's slightly damp now where her swimsuit has soaked through her shorts. She should get up and go back to them.

They met at a conversation class at the Institut Français. That was a year ago now. She joined because it had been some-thing to do during lockdown, a daily practice on Duolingo, the ladder of the leaderboard, a way of measuring the days. Sometimes when her flat – little more than a bedsit, really, the galley kitchen not even quite a separate room – felt for all its bijou size too empty, too lonely, she'd gone to sleep with Michel Thomas playing over Spotify, or with her phone streaming a random French radio station. Afterwards, it seemed a nice thing to try to keep up the momentum, to do it properly, consolidate it all. The Institut had a programme of cultural events too – an art deco listed library, an art deco Ciné Lumière – and she liked the idea of reading books, of watching arthouse films, in a beautiful space.

There hadn't been an immediate spark between them: when she set her tote bag down on the free desk next to him, he was just a random middle-aged man, brown eyes that crinkled when he smiled hello, dark brown, but mainly greying hair. Hair in no sort of particular style – too long, maybe, a bit mullety, as if he was overdue a haircut, but even that she barely registered. She couldn't have told you what he was wearing: a jumper maybe, darkish? But because they happened to be sitting at adjacent desks in that first session, and because the teacher asked them to keep those seats in subsequent weeks to make it easier for her to remember names, that was that: they were conversation partners.

'Comment vous appelez-vous?' they asked each other dutifully, that first class.

'Je m'appelle Beatrice.'

'Je m'appelle Justin.'

He extended his hand, then withdrew it: 'Sorry, we're not supposed to do that any more, are we?'

'Bumping elbows somehow doesn't seem very French.'

'No, it doesn't, does it?'

They smiled at each other, awkward, polite.

The teacher had written a list of topics and suggested questions on the whiteboard, in the stereotypical French handwriting she remembered from school: round and curly.

'Ok,' he said. 'Let's do this. D'où venez-vous?'

'Je viens de Belfast. D'Irlande du Nord,' she said, conscious of how flat, how Belfast, her voice sounded. Her French teacher in school had had a strong Belfast accent, and they'd all joked about learning a French that no one outside of Northern Ireland could ever understand. His accent, on the other hand, sounded very smoothly French. 'D'où venez-vous?' she made herself ask. *Doo venny voo?*

'Je viens d'un petit village en Sussex. Ce n'est pas très intéressant.'

'Qu'est-ce que vous faites?'

'Je suis analyste. Je travaille dans une banque.'

'Je travaille— How do you say publishing?'

'Vous travaillez dans une maison d'édition? Bon. Et où habitez-vous?'

'J'habite dans une petite, I don't know what the word is, bedsit? à Tooting Bec. Où habitez-vous?'

'J'habite dans une maison à Stockwell. Alors, famille.'

'Je suis – is enfant seule how you say it? Ma mère habite toujours à Belfast. Et vous?'

'J'habite avec mes trois filles. Elles s'appellent Monique, Léa et Elodie. Ma femme est mourie.'

They were meant to be taking notes, to describe their partner to the rest of the group. 'Sorry,' she said, 'let me just get those names again. Monique . . .'

'L, e-with-an-accent, a, and Elodie.'

'Monique, Léa et Elodie – and votre femme s'appelle Maureen?'

'No – sorry, I said, "Ma femme est mourie." How do you say it. Mourir. Morte. Elle est morte. She died five years ago.'

'Oh! Oh goodness. Oh I'm so sorry.'

'Thank you. Elle est morte: I'm sure there must be a very basic Freudian reason why I can't get that straight.'

'No no, of course. Ok.' She crossed out *Maureen*. Her pen hovered, stupidly, over the page. *Elle est morte.*

'I'm sorry,' she said again. 'How did she—'

But he was already talking. 'She was actually French,' he said. 'My French was so bad, though, we only ever spoke English together. I thought it would be good to learn it properly so I could speak it with Elodie. Her mother tongue, and all that.'

'Your French is really good. I mean your accent and all. Mine's just Duolingo. I can read it ok, I can understand it when I hear it, but when it comes to speaking I have no idea.' She felt herself gabbling.

'En français, s'il vous plaît,' the teacher said, and they went back – with relief, she thought – to the list of questions.

Finally the teacher clapped her hands. 'Alors. Terminez vos conversations.'

'Shall I say or not?' she said, hurriedly, awkward. 'About your wife. I mean when I have to summarise you to the group.'

'You can say,' he said. 'Thank you for asking. But I find it easier to say it upfront, I think, so that people know that about me. Rather than prolonging the moment when it inevitably comes out.'

'It must be – very hard.'

'Elodie has never known her,' he said. 'That's perhaps the hardest thing.'

'I never knew my dad,' she said. 'He was – well, I never really knew who he was. Mum always used to tell me different stories. Make up cards from him on my birthday, with all these exotic stamps that I found out later she got off the internet. I know that's not the same. But—'

'Dans cette salle, on ne parle que français!' said the teacher, mock-sternly.

'I'm sorry,' he said a moment later, under his breath.

'No, no,' she whispered back. 'I used to think it was really cool – really special.'

For the rest of the lesson, then, they were reserved, polite; kept entirely to French.

After the sessions, the teacher encouraged them to go with her to the pub round the corner, an old-man boozer where she looked incongruous, her peroxide hair and mascara and impeccable lipstick, her leather skirt and boots. About half of them went regularly, sipping their pints or their glasses of wine and talking in self-conscious French. Justin never came. The twelve weeks passed, and then the final class, when they each had to pass a little examination, and received a certificate. She had been inordinately nervous about having to converse with the teacher in front of everyone, and felt a ridiculous flood of relief to have passed, to be told she could progress to the Advanced class. She felt herself beaming as she walked back to her desk, and as he stood up to let her pass, they hugged.

'Félicitations, mademoiselle.'

'Merci, monsieur.'

That day he came to the pub with them. Almost every-one came, and there were too many of them, squeezed in to their usual booth. As he hovered with his mini-bottle of red wine, she inched over to try to make space for him beside her, at the very edge of the bench. There really wasn't enough room, his thigh was pressed right against hers.

'You never come for a drink afterwards,' she said. 'I mean, vous jamais . . . come here,' she finished, flustered, laughing.

'Monique a seize ans, samedi dernier,' he said. 'Alors, j'ai enfin un babysitter. Et elle m'a dit que je dois sortir. So that I meet someone,' he added, drinking back his glass of wine and pouring the rest of the little bottle in.

'And – vous voulez rencontrer quelqu'un?' she said.

'J'ai eu des relations, de temps en temps.'

They were both talking in low voices, and under the general clamour of the table it was hard to hear him.

'Sorry,' she said. 'I didn't quite . . .'

'I have' – and she almost felt him blush – 'met people. Slept with people. Occasionally. But nothing—'

They were pressed too close together to be able to look directly at each other as they talked. She realised her heart had slowed, almost to a halt, and was now going again, very fast.

'Rien ne vaut la peine d'en parler à votre fille?' she said, carefully.

'Exactement,' he said.

'But you're here now.'

'I'm here now,' he said, and held out his glass. His wrist bare where his shirt was rolled up. His glass trembling slightly. It was hardly any movement at all for her to reach out and touch hers to his.

'You're still sad,' he says later, as they're dressing for dinner. He moves the mass of her wet hair over one shoulder, does up the tricky button of her blue dress.

'I'm sorry,' she says. 'I'm fine really. It's just – you know.'

He turns her to face him, tilts her face upwards with his finger. Regards her for a moment, then leans to kiss her forehead lightly. As he might do to one of his daughters, she thinks. She puts a hand to his chest, the greying hair where his white linen shirt is unbuttoned. It never really occurred to her before that all the hair on your body turned grey – even your pubic hair. She runs her hand lightly upwards, his collarbones, over his shoulders, which slope; he is a slight man, and barely any taller than her. He has the body of a cyclist – the hours spent on his Brompton to and from the office every day, on his racing bike at the weekend, racking up hundreds of miles. Taut and slim-hipped, boyish. She puts both hands to his face, traces the fine edge of his jawline, ever so slightly softened, but not yet slackening. A fleck of toilet paper from a fresh shaving cut: she licks her finger and taps it off. He's not old, not yet; she's gone thirty now, not exactly young.

'You're thinking I'm old,' he says with a grimace.

'I'm actually not!' she says. 'I was actually thinking you weren't.'

'I will be,' he says. 'In four years I'll be fifty. I tell myself sometimes, I'm fifteen years older than you. *Fifteen*. It sounds terrible, like that. But with you, Bea – I don't feel too old not to start again. Wait,' he says. 'I think there were too many negatives in that sentence. I don't feel so old that I couldn't. If you will. Whatever your mother may have said about me. About us.'

'Mum said nothing much about anything,' she says. 'It

was just the drink talking.' Then she says, impulsively, 'She calls you Captain von Trapp.'

He bursts out laughing. To her surprise, her relief, she finds herself laughing too.

'See, this is why you're never going to meet my mother,' she says. 'She's always trying to undermine me.'

She realises, as she says it, that she sounds exactly like her mother.

'I reckon I could handle your mother,' he says, smiling. 'Why don't you let me try?'

'Because—' she says. 'Just because.'

'You're sweet to worry about me,' he says, 'but I'll be fine. We'll be fine. You and me, Bea.'

There are just three full days of their holiday left. They go back to Jemaa el-Fnaa, to visit the souks this time, but Elodie suddenly decides she wants to go on a ride in one of the horse-drawn carriages that line the Lalla Hasna gardens. He shrugs and agrees, starts looking for someone to negotiate a price with. But Monique and Léa are mutinous.

'Look at the horses,' Monique says. 'Just look at them.'

Some of the pairs are in decent shape – on the thin side, but with glossy coats and well-brushed manes and tails. But others, it's true, are in pretty bad condition. Open sores on their knees and ankles, painfully jutting hipbones and ribs.

'We're not doing it, Dad,' says Monique. 'No way.'

'No way,' echoes Léa.

Elodie, pink-cheeked, crosses her arms over her little butterfly-print playsuit, frowns and pouts and then begins to cry.

'But I want a horsey ride,' she says. 'I want a horsey ride *so* badly.'

'Look, Elly,' says Monique, kneeling beside her. 'Look at the poor horseys. They don't feed them enough – they whip them. Look at their poor sore legs. You don't want to make them pull you round in a heavy carriage in the hot sun, do you?'

But he has already started negotiations with several of the drivers, who are trying to usher them towards different carriages.

'Dad,' says Léa. 'Dad, tell them you've changed your mind.'

'Don't worry,' he says, distractedly, 'we'll make sure we get a good-looking pair.'

'No,' Monique says. 'We're not going. Dad, we're not doing it.'

'For heaven's sake,' he says. 'It's just for half an hour around the gardens.'

'Nope,' says Monique, and Léa echoes her: 'Not doing it.'

'I want a horsey ride,' Elodie wails.

'Come on,' he says. 'I'm not leaving you two here alone.'

Then Monique says, 'Ok. Family vote.'

'Yeah,' says Léa. 'Family vote.'

They turn to her.

'Me and Léa vote no,' says Monique, 'and Dad and Elly vote yes. What do you vote?'

'Nikki,' he says. 'That's hardly fair.'

'Is she part of this family or not?'

'It's not fair to ask her like that. I'm asking *you*, Nikki. I'm asking you to – get off your own high horse, and do something nice for your sister. I don't see what the big deal is. It's just half an hour.'

'It's the principle,' Monique says, arms folded.

'Jesus Christ,' he says. 'I'll give the driver some extra dirham, ok, tell him to buy the horses some carrots.'

'You're pathetic, Dad,' says Monique. 'Buy them some carrots – you're so patronising.'

She feels him take a breath. He turns to Elodie, tries to promise her a wooden snake that moves, a beautiful box for her treasures, a bracelet from the souk, instead. But all she wants is a ride in a horse-drawn carriage.

A bigger group of drivers has gathered round now, gesticulating, imploring. People are stopping to look at them.

'Two for, two against,' Monique says again. 'Whose side are you on? You've got to choose.'

She takes a breath herself. 'I don't think it's right,' she says, 'the condition of some of the horses.'

'Thank you!' says Monique.

'But,' she says. 'But. I think that this is something Elodie really wants, so I think – I think we should just do it, and, as your dad says, choose a healthy-looking pair . . .'

'Yes,' he says. 'Right, let's do this.'

'You're a traitor,' says Monique. 'You are such a traitor.'

'Monique! Don't you dare talk to her like that.'

'Monique's just saying it like it is,' says Léa.

'She knows it's wrong,' says Monique. 'You know, Beatrice. And instead you're just trying to please my dad. I thought Dad was pathetic but I don't even have words for how pathetic you are. You make me sick. Both of you. You both make me sick to my stomach' – and then Monique unleashes a stream of vicious French, invective that she wouldn't have a hope of understanding even with years of dogged conversation classes; but whose feeling is so clear, she doesn't need to.

They end up getting a taxi back to the kasbah – no horse ride, no souk. Monique and Léa take themselves off to their room. Elodie is still so upset she refuses to eat.

She sits alone in the restaurant, waiting for him to coax the children to join them, or to come alone. She wonders if she should be doing something. She thinks: What am I doing?

He apologises, later in bed, for the family drama, for the way she was caught up in it.

'The loss of Camille made us closer in many ways,' he says, 'Monique and Léa especially, and I'm so proud of how they are with Elly. They had to grow up fast, and in many ways they're far beyond their years. But you have to remember, they're still teenagers. Well, Nikki is, and Léa will be all too soon. And we have our ups and downs like any family.'

She thinks: You hardly ever use her name any more. And she thinks, the automatic *we* of your family excludes me: as of course it does. As of course it should.

She thinks, then, of the first time she went to his house. He'd been back to hers a couple of times, and she'd met the children by then, but going to their home was something different, a new level of significance. The Swedish nanny had opened the door – tall, blonde, competent; younger than her, but with the advantage of being in her domain. As she put on her coat and gathered her things the nanny kept up a belligerently detailed account of the day – the substitutions of the Ocado order that afternoon, a notice about gas works to be carried out on the street, the dish-washer still malfunctioning – and the thought went through her mind: had she been one of his *des relations*?

The nanny had left dinner for them – a sort of creamy potato dish, dotted with anchovies, salmon fillets wrapped in parchment ready to be baked, a lemony salad. As it cooked, she sat feeling awkward at the kitchen island, chaotic with piles of post and charger cables and Elodie's drawings. There were family photographs everywhere you looked, in frames and on the fridge and in a collage on one of the kitchen walls. His wife, whom she'd imagined as glossy-haired with red lipstick, was in fact pixie-like, a snaggle-toothed smile with a cropped haircut. In more than one of the photos she was in Birkenstocks, with a baby in a cloth wrap sling. In one of the photos her hair was blue – in another, pink. In one of them she had a glitter moon and stars on the side of her face.

She felt foolish then. It was still early on enough that she was assiduously asking about his wife, and so she doggedly commented on the photographs, so as not to be *not* commenting on them, and it was a relief when the salmon was cooked and the children were called.

For a while after that, she wondered whether she and Camille would have got on – would have liked each other. Except that she couldn't think of the circumstances in which they ever would have met. Camille had been a set designer, and they still had some of her best model boxes in the loft, and from time to time, if Elodie was sad, she was allowed, under careful supervision by her sisters, to move around the furniture and the figurines, like a doll's house.

Neither of them has said anything for a while now, and she wonders if they're wandering the same rooms in their thoughts. In some ways, it has seemed as if she could slot easily into their lives. The only furniture she actually owns is Ikea, lots of it second-hand from Gumtree anyway. Her clothes would fit easily into his wall-to-wall wardrobes, empty now of the clothes of his wife's that were either given to charity or subsumed into the wardrobes of Monique and Léa. Her books, the only thing of any real substance or quantity that she has, could go anywhere. The box-room off the landing could be her study. She would have a nice lamp – plants. Make it cosy. Read manuscripts in the garden. Sleeping and waking not just occasionally but every day in his bedroom, in his bed. They have discussed it. They were in her flat that evening, and as they were lying there, after they'd made love, before he had to leave, because he never stayed the whole night at hers, he said, 'I want more than anything for you to be happy', and for an awful moment she thought it was the prelude to breaking up with her.

When she realised what he meant, that he was talking about her moving in with him, she started to cry.

'No no,' he said, 'oh no', and he brushed away her tears with his thumbs, 'Oh Bea', and she felt grown-up and brimful with tenderness at their consideration for each other. It was true, she thought: in that moment she would have emptied out all of herself to make him happy too. It hadn't mattered then – his baggage, as her friends ironically called it. She reminds herself that nothing, objectively speaking, has changed.

The next morning, the five of them eat breakfast together as if the previous day didn't happen, or has been forgotten, and discuss what to do for their final two days. Although she'd love to go back to Jemaa el-Fnaa, to the medina, to the souk, she doesn't dare mention it. The girls want to stay by the pool, and swim, and sunbathe. She smiles, agrees. But he insists that she does something purely for herself, and so after breakfast they go to book a hammam at the private spa on the kasbah's estate, the full version: hammam au savon noir avec gommage.

The hammam baths are in a low, secluded building, made in the traditional style, rough clay walls mixed with straw. Inside, the rooms are tiled, and lit only by candles in lanterns. Incense is burning in censers, intoxicating, soporific. A woman leads her to the changing room, explains with smiles and gestures and in broken French that she must take off all of her clothes, fold and place them *here*, tie on this piece of fabric *so*. When she is ready, the woman takes her to the bath. She sits on a heated marble slab while the woman pours rapid bowls of warm water over her, soaps her, rinses her again, pastes her in a eucalyptus-scented oil then leaves her to lie down. The room is still; the heat rises. She lies on her front, then turns onto her back; closes her eyes. She could not say how much time passes. She feels herself breathing more deeply than she maybe has done in days.

When the woman comes back, it is with an exfoliating mitt. The woman removes the piece of fabric around her hips, then up and down each of her limbs, her back, her chest, her stomach, her buttocks, she scrubs her, harder than she would ever have thought to scrub herself. Dead skin comes off in swathes, fat grey worms, which the woman sluices off approvingly.

'L'ancienne toi,' the woman says, gesturing, her face an exaggerated scowl. 'Bientôt, tout sera nouvelle.' When she's exfoliated to the woman's satisfaction, the woman sits her up and motions for her to bend forward so that she can wash her hair. She bends, releasing her hair from its topknot to fall forward, feeling the nape of her neck exposed. The woman pours warm water over her head, again, again, then rubs her scalp and hair with soap, her fingers strong, pours water, more water, soaps again. The water is streaming down into her ears, over her eyes, into her nose and mouth – she can hardly breathe. Although the woman is being paid to do this, although she is paying the woman, hers is the humble pose, submissive, ancient, biblical. It feels unbearably intimate, this woman, this fully clothed stranger, soaping and rinsing her hair while she sits naked, helpless. No one has done this for her since she was a child, probably. She feels suddenly overcome with how much she misses her own mother. She misses her mother so much that she wonders if it is her mother she is actually missing.

Afterwards, the woman dries her with a towel, rubs thick rose-scented lotion all over, leads her to lie in a dimly lit antechamber, brings her sweet mint tea and a plate of dates. She drinks in tiny sips until the little glass is empty, eats the dates, fat and almost liquid themselves, then lies back, gazes at the ceiling, a series of arches and half-domes tiled in intricate patterns, a brass lamp with stained-glass panels suspended at the highest central point.

She remembers a story of six men searching for God – a story her mother had told her, it must have been when she started primary school, when she asked why they didn't go to church like most people in her class. Of the six men in the story, one said that God was yellow – another was adamant that He was orange. Three others started fighting because God was evidently blue, purple, green. The last man slaughtered them all because they were heretics: God was obviously red. But they were all, her mother had said, looking through their own little square of a stained-glass lamp. God was all of it at once – more than they could ever know, and they were each blinded by the fear of all they could not know. She doesn't know why she thinks of it now.

She lies there for a long time, waiting for the woman or for someone from the reception desk to fetch her, but no one comes. Eventually she gets up and makes her way back down the lantern-lit corridor to the changing room, retrieves her dress and sandals from the cubbyhole, gets dressed and goes outside.

The midday sun is hot on her skin, which suddenly feels vulnerable, exposed. It is too northern, too pale, to be without factor 50. She hasn't brought a hat, or sunglasses. She walks back to the kasbah the long way, in the shade, along the dusty path between the pomegranate trees, the hibiscus: there is wild hibiscus growing everywhere.

She loves him, she tells herself. He doesn't want a baby, but then, probably nor does she. He is older than her, but then, so what? They say *je t'aime* in the language of his dead wife, which is kind of fucked up, but on the other hand, is the language they met each other in: it is their language too. If this isn't what she had in any abstract sense wished for, what of the way life turns out ever is?

They are at the big pool, splashing and laughing. She sits down on the edge of a lounger, under the rattan umbrella. Everything, even the tops of her feet, feels almost painfully tenderised.

'Bibi's back!' shouts Elodie.

'Was that good?' he calls out from the far side of the pool. 'Was it all it's talked up to be, do you feel born again?' But before she can answer, he dives under and capsizes the lilo, toppling Léa and Monique shrieking into the water.

'Play Lilo Shark with us,' Elodie shouts. 'Come on, play Lilo Shark!'

'It doesn't feel right to jump straight into chlorine now,' she says. 'I'm going to sit this one out.'

She sits and watches them, him and the three of them, splashing and playing and laughing. How can she ever have imagined herself into their life?

For all the sunshine, she feels suddenly cold. *Mal dans ma peau*, she thinks. She shivers again and wonders, almost with relief, if she might be coming down with something.

But he is the one who gets ill. A dodgy tummy: he's up most of the night. When he crawls into bed, sunken-eyed and sour-breathed between bouts of vomiting, she strokes his hair back from his clammy forehead and thinks how quickly illness reshapes our features, turns us into intimations of the death mask of ourselves.

'Shh, now,' she murmurs, 'shh, now. You're ok – you're ok.'

His heart is skittering. His breathing is shallow, effortful.

She thinks of what it must mean to nurse someone that you love through the end of life, to death. How you ever come back from that yourself.

She must seem incredibly facile to him, she thinks: naive, and young. Then she thinks, with a pang of great sadness, that that's what he likes about her.

By the morning his stomach and bowels still haven't settled. She wakes to hear him groaning in the toilet: the splash of his defecation, that awful heave and groan again. She didn't know before that pity for someone you love can make you love them even more. She had always assumed it would be the opposite: a diminishing, a disgust. She realises it with a sort of dismay.

She gets Elodie up and dressed, rouses the older girls, takes everyone to breakfast.

'Is Daddy going to die?' Elodie asks.

'Of course not. He's just got a bad tummy.'

'He will die one day,' Léa says. 'We all will.'

'Yes,' she says, 'but your daddy is so fit and healthy, he's not going to die for a very long time.'

'You can't know that.'

'No,' she says. 'None of us can ever know much, really.'

She suddenly feels very weary.

Léa looks at her. Puffy-faced, hair going every which way. Léa is at the age she remembers hating most: neither one thing nor another.

'I know things,' says Léa. 'I know loads of things.'

'What will happen to us if Daddy dies too?' Elodie says.

Even Monique has put down her phone and is looking at her now.

'Your daddy's not going to die,' she says firmly. 'It's just a silly dodgy tummy. Now come on. *We're* going to enjoy every second of our last day.'

She sprays sunscreen carefully all over Elodie and Léa, over the parts of Monique's back that she can't reach herself, smooths it thoroughly in. She orchestrates game after game of Lilo Shark, of underwater challenges, races. The day goes more slowly than any day has yet. As midday approaches, she makes the girls get out of the sun and fully under the umbrellas. She plays My Little Pony with Elodie, making nests for the ponies under the loungers, feeding them leaves. After a while, Elodie clambers up onto her lounger and nestles in beside her, sucking her thumb.

'Bibi,' Elodie says. 'If you and Daddy get married, do I have to call you Mummy?'

'You don't have to call me anything,' she says.

'Because she's not our mummy,' Léa says.

'None of you has to call me Mummy.'

Elodie thinks. 'What if I *want* to call you Mummy?'

'Well,' she says, 'I don't know. But you can still call me Bibi. You're the only person who's ever called me Bibi.'

'I am?' Elodie is pleased with this. 'Bibi,' she says, touching her nose, as if christening her. She pokes her nose harder. 'Bibi,' she says. 'You look funny like that. Let's play Funny Faces', and for a while they do, gurning and gawping at each other. Then Elodie says, 'Do you love Daddy?'

The question has come out of nowhere, but she is aware of Monique listening behind her sunglasses, magazine poised. Monique, too thin for her body, for the shape of her face, her bones. Léa is listening too: Léa with her hair cut too short to suit her, in defiance of incipient adolescence, or in homage to her mother, she isn't sure, and maybe nor is Léa. She feels a great softening towards them.

'Yes,' she says, carefully. 'Yes, I love your daddy.'

'Are you going to get married?'

'I don't know.'

'But if he asks you, you have to say yes.'

Elodie doesn't seem to consider it a question.

She strokes the child's hair. The drone of the bees, the rise and fall of the noise of the crickets, the pulse of the sun . . . Soon, Elodie is asleep. She tries to adjust her own body where it's pressed against the arm of the lounger – tries to adjust the child's limbs to make sure that all of her skin is out of the sun. She is heavy: far heavier in sleep than if you lift her in real life, somehow. Her own legs start to prickle and fizz with the beginnings of cramp, but she doesn't move. She wonders how it must feel to love a child so much that you give your own life for them, even when they are just in the abstract, not yet born – even when you're the mother of two other children who need you too, who arguably have both less but also more of a claim on you.

That was the horror of it: the cancer that killed Camille had been an aggressive one, hormonal, exacerbated by the hormones of pregnancy, but the treatment would have been at the expense of that pregnancy, and she had refused it. She had delivered the baby early, as early as was safely viable, in the hope that there would still be time to save her, but there hadn't been.

Even knowing that, she wonders, would Camille still have chosen the same?

She wonders what it will mean for Elodie, as she grows up, the knowledge of the burden of such love, the awful knowledge that the love was never about you in any personal sort of a sense.

And she wonders about love's depths and reaches, if it's something of which we're all capable. It has to be, surely, if there's to be hope for any of us.

A peacock screeches right behind them, startling them all. Elodie stirs. Monique starts laughing, squabbling with Léa about who jumped most. Elodie sits up, frowning, and her limbs rush with the pain of release. The peacock screeches again, then again, such a sharp and penetrating scream, part keening, part alarm, and first Léa, then Elodie, then Monique start imitating it, and after a moment she joins in – not caring, in that moment, what anyone might think, all of them throwing back their heads, making wild and ever wilder sounds, calling something in, or letting something go.

Lay Me Down

WE WERE AT A CHRISTMAS DRINKS PARTY. Or rather: we were two floors above where the Christmas drinks party was happening. Our toddler wanted to be with the other kids, in the attic playroom, but the flights of stairs were beyond her, or beyond our capacity to relax while we thought of her tumbling down them, so the attic playroom it was.

We didn't both need to be there. But where my husband was I wanted to be, which I suppose was saying something.

Our toddler was happy enough, beavering around after our friends' kids, playing with our friends' kids' toys with a commitment she never showed to her own, near-identical versions.

We, meanwhile, were playing a competitive version of Where's Wally? which went like this. One person selected a page, and timed with their phone's stopwatch the other person finding Wally. The first two times, my husband found Wally in under thirty seconds, while I gave up after four then three minutes.

You either get it within the first minute or you've no hope, I said.

Interesting theory.

Well, then, what's your technique? I asked.

I look for the one, he said, that looks like Wally.

And he hadn't even meant it to be funny.

Are you ok? he said.

Flip me I love you, I said, when I'd stopped choking on my laughter.

Are you pissed already? he said.

We'd both watched Jason, our host (or half of them), lashing most of a bottle of vodka into the mulled wine, then shrugging and adding the rest. We'd looked at each other, but then, screw it, we'd both drunk it anyway.

Probably, I said.

There was something Marguerite Duras had said, I thought, that knowledge of sexual relationship was there either from the beginning, or not at all. Or something. We'd been through so much – I mean, who hadn't, in our case twelve years and three kids – and we were such good friends now, that we had to remember that.

Why don't we slip into a spare room for two minutes, I said, and—

You really are pissed. Don't you be having any more of that stuff.

He went to take my glass, probably only half in jest. I surrendered.

There's a non-alcoholic version too, you know, he said.

It's not *non-alcoholic*, I said, it's *alcohol-free*. It's a positive thing, not defined by its negativity. Like carefree, footloose-and-fancy-free. Like the way you don't say *child-less* these days, you say *child-free*.

On cue, our eight-year-old barrelled into the room, followed by our ten-year-old, and someone else's, and someone else's again, all Shloer-crazy. In what world did we have a ten-year-old? In what world had we decided, just as our youngest was in P1 and we were starting to get our lives back, that it would be a good idea to have another? Had it been love, or fear?

Oh Lord. Here we were. This was us. This was it: what we got. This was our *life*.

I look for the one that looks like Wally.

Was it bad parenting, I wondered, to send your ten-year-old down then back up three flights of stairs to bring you a top-up of spiked mulled wine?

Should we try to go downstairs again? I said.

She'll only gurn. You go, if you want.

Jason was my husband's oldest friend: another one of the cream of Ulster, as Junior Master Mr Samuel Beckett had famously called the Campbell College boys, adding, for clarification, *rich and thick.*

It's ok, I said, you go. Just don't get stuck with the guy with the antlers.

The guy with the antlers was always at Jason and Aisha's parties, though not, obviously, always in antlers. He and his wife had three kids too, all girls, all always dressed the same, right down to their hairstyles, right down to the colour of the clips in their hair. There was a desperation to his antics (*antics*: I thought, *noun, plural,* a purportedly quirky habit of wearing a reindeer headband through the festive season). A desperation too, of course, to his performative drinking, though what was it someone else had said? – *that which we despise most in others* . . .

I was no good at parties any more. I got drunk on one glass and talked in quotes I only half-remembered.

On you go, I said. Go on! Being serious. I need to work on my Wally-location skills.

My husband smiled, got off his hunkers to his feet, mock-groaning. There was that funny thing where, if you'd met someone in your twenties, you sort of always saw them that way, their older selves just layered on. Or maybe it was the other way around: the memory of their younger self always surfacing. Either way, he was looking well, I thought. Tired but handsome. One of Jason and Aisha's friends, maybe the woman with daughters whose name I had to try better to remember, would probably flirt with him, and that would only be a good thing.

I love you, I said as he left, and I meant it.

Outside the curtainless window, it was mizzling. The dark shape of the monkey-puzzle tree in the garden, faintly sinister in the dusk. The bare branches of the lime and chestnut trees on the Earlswood Road beyond, swaying patiently. Maybe, I thought, this all really had once been some earl's wood. James Hamilton, 1st Viscount Clandeboye, who'd taken vast tracts of County Down in the seventeenth century. Or Conn O'Neill, he of Connswater, the river – well, and present-day shopping centre. The *Earl's Wood*, the way the Donegall Pass, where I'd gone for music lessons twice a week for years, had actually, literally been one of six passes cut through his forest by Lord Donegall, so that people could more easily get to the south of the town.

You started to find yourself interested in that sort of thing as you got older, I thought. Who had the people been who came before. It was when you began to realise, maybe, that one day you'd be one of them. I'd been looking at a book of photographs of old Belfast by Robert French that morning, 1890s people queuing on the jetty off Queen's Island to catch the paddle steamer to Bangor for the day, return fare of 1s 6d or concession 1s, the caption said. Looking at them, giddy in their finery, the pleasure boat and treats of the day to come (dulse, yellow-man, the penny machines, a poke), you couldn't help thinking just how far from their minds it would have been that they were the people of the past, that the world was rapidly moving on around and without them, and they hadn't even realised it yet.

I felt a bit like that yesterday passing the Christmas market, my husband said when I said this to him.

Very funny, I said, though it sort of was. He didn't think about death, at least not in the ways I did. We're here now, he said, which was exactly the thing I'd to constantly remind myself. In the photographs, everyone, but everyone, male and female, and even most of the little boys, were wearing hats. You thought of the hatters and milliners then, how it must have seemed the stablest of trades, until all of a sudden people stopped wearing headgear, almost overnight, it must have seemed, when before it would have been unthinkable to be in public without covering your head. I often thought of that: of unforeseeable obsolescence. Video rental shops, for example. London A–Zs. Alarm clocks. You could do the history of a generation in suddenly-obsolete things. Floppy disks. MP3 players. Camera film, and one-hour processing labs. Tamagotchis. Hair mascara, for which you either saved up your babysitting money or else nicked, from the Debenhams in CastleCourt. Body glitter! When that arrived from America, by way of Claire's Accessories, we thought we were living the dream.

But who were we, our generation, if you could even call it that? We weren't the previous generation, but nor were we the one almost immediately after, the one people called the *ceasefire babies*. Who were we, and what had we done? We'd gone away, mostly, those of us who could, and then we'd come back, or started to, when we realised there wasn't really anywhere else. I'd gone to Manchester, my husband, defying his Campbell College posh-boy peers (St Andrews, Durham, Bristol), had chosen East Anglia. We'd then met during a miserable year in London – miserable individually, though less miserable, mercifully, together – and stuck out our respective flatshares and then shared bedroom for a further two before taking the plunge and moving back – and we said the word with an audible *quote unquote* – home.

And now we had a son sitting the Transfer Test and another almost as tall as him and a daughter who bossed us all about, as well as friends-from-home moving back at a rate of knots. Or at least at the rate of Flybe, who advertised their planes with the slogan *Faster than road or rail*, to which you always felt tempted to add the unspoken, though implicit, *but only just.*

Jason and Aisha had swapped East London for East Belfast just this summer, in time for their elder girl to start school. They'd bought this house – a vast run-down former something-home – for less than the price of their two-bed London flat with its boxy one-and-a-half-metre balcony, or so they never stopped telling us, whether boasting or apologising we weren't quite sure. They now talked about Ballyhackamore and the Belmont Road with the zeal of the convert, or at least the desperation of those hoping against hope they didn't wake up one morning to find, square-metreage and garden notwithstanding, they'd made a huge mistake. Or maybe it should be the zeal of the *revert.* Jason had – if only nominally – converted to Islam in order to marry Aisha, for her family's sake, and they called it *reverting*, which I kind of quite liked, as if *it* had always been there and it was you who'd just finally come to your senses. It all seemed to be going ok, so far. Aisha hadn't even had any of the well-are-you-a-Protestant-Muslim-or-a-Catholic-one jokes. Though to call that a joke, even ironically, would technically and maybe even legally be an abuse of the word.

I liked Aisha a lot. She was a secret smoker and a terrible

cook. For this last reason alone, she loved Northern Ireland: the land of the traybake, in philosophy and practice impossible to fuck up. She couldn't believe you just mashed it all up a bit, put it in a tin and chilled it. Un-fuck-up-able, she said. Or un-fuckable-up.

Hey.

Oh, I said, turning. Hi. It was Jason. Sorry, I said. Miles away. I checked for my daughter, who'd been, I realised with a start, suspiciously quiet. It was ok, or rather she was, if not the playroom around her: she was methodically shredding a whole box of tissues into tiny snowflake-like pieces. Sorry, I said again.

No worries, he said. Good party?

Yeah, no, class, I said automatically, before realising he was probably being sarcastic. For some of us, anyway, I said, sarcastically too, then added: Sorry about your playroom.

He looked slightly vaguely at the tissue-snow. No worries. Cleaner'll sort it tomorrow.

He rubbed at his head. Jason had been really good-looking once, all cheekbones and floppy curtained hair. If you liked that sort of thing. But his hair was receding at the temples now, and thinning on top, and the cheekbones had sort of receded somehow too, or the rest of his face had whatever the opposite of receded was. Accumulated? Advanced? Countering my earlier theory entirely, I had a sudden vision of him at fifty, or sixty, or whatever, for us, would count as middle-aged. Catch yourself on, I thought. You *are* middle-aged. You are, probably literally, and that's if you're *lucky*, right now in the exact statistical middle of your life.

You ok? he said.

What? No, yeah, grand, I said. Just . . .

I gestured out the window.

. . . thinking, I finished, lamely. Like if this was a film, I heard myself saying, a Christmas film, there would be snow. But all's we get is rain.

So says the Confucius of Connswater, he said. What? What is it?

Conn and his water, I said. I was just thinking about him there. About who he might have been. Whether all this once was his.

Is his grave not up for sale or something? Jason said. I think I read that somewhere. Or what they think might be his grave. The last King of Castlereagh. It's just up by my folks. Off the Holywood Road. Planning permission for half a dozen houses, or something.

I didn't know that, I said.

Yeah, no, I'm pretty sure.

Neither of us said anything more for a moment.

All's we get is rain, he said.

I liked Jason. I liked him well enough. Or minded him less than most of my husband's friends. And since they'd moved here, he and Aisha and their girls were ninety per cent of our social life. Or what passed for it.

I'm a veritable fount, I said, of what would you call it – Confusion?

That made him smile.

You, he said, nodding at my glass, need a top-up, missus.

He was holding a bottle, which turned out to be Goats do Roam. Who bought that stuff, I'd always wondered. Apparently, we did. Or at least we drank it. He topped up my glass, right to the brim. Winked at me.

Cheers, you.

Cheers, I said.

We touched glasses; drank.

Daddy! His daughter Sufia was at the door. Here, Daddy, come *on*!

A handful of months, and her accent pure Belfast already.

Honest to goodness, Daddy, she said. She whirled in a circle and darted off.

I'm coming, Jason said. He turned back to me. I'm putting on a film for the rug-rats. He added, So I am. It was the way we'd started to talk: saying the things we'd once said, and would probably still say anyway, ironically.

What are you screening? I said.

Wait for it. Are you ready? *Frozen . . . 2.*

Wait, what, she survives?

Jason didn't get my joke. To be fair, it wasn't my finest.

Oh, just let it go, I said. This time he smiled.

Here's one Sufia likes, he said. How does Olaf get around Arendelle.

How, I said. How does Olaf get around Arendelle.

On an ice-cycle.

Very funny.

Jason wasn't exactly standing close, but it was close

enough that I could tell he smelled of weed. He and my husband had apparently been stoners back in the day, the flat they shared in Norwich, stories of munchie-sessions, of legendary hash brownies that knocked you out for eighteen hours straight. It wasn't my sort of thing, and hadn't been either of theirs since they moved to London and started work for law firms, Jason as an actual lawyer, my husband in IT.

Do I reek of it? he said. Is it really that obvious?

What? I said. I hadn't said anything.

Half a mile up the road, he said, I used to hide my smoking from my parents. Now I hide it from my kids.

And Aisha? I said.

As soon as I'd said her name, I was glad I had.

Jason looked at me. Then he laughed. It wasn't a mean laugh. It was a laugh like he almost felt sorry for me.

It's not like she doesn't not know, he said.

I was still parsing the double-negatives when my daughter, who'd finally run out of tissues, or stamina, cannonballed at me. I picked her up: glad of the weight of her, the solidity. The excuse.

Lolo want milk, she said.

Okey-doke, I said. Let's get this Chloe some milk.

Downstairs (down stairs and stairs) the party was in full swing, or as full-to-swing as a Sunday afternoon on the Earlswood Road seemed likely to get. The boys were in the den, where they'd located Jason's Xbox, and were embroiled in a game of *FIFA*-something. In the kitchen, Aisha, bless her, even if he was her neighbour and so technically her responsibility, was indulging Antler-man, and looked to have been doing so for quite some time already. I got Chloe her milk, plonked her on a beanbag with her brothers, then went to find my husband. He was in the living room by the fire, indeed flirting with the mother of the three-girls-in-dresses. Their cheeks were rosy, with alcohol, or heat, or novelty. I went up to him and took his arm, kissed his pink cheek. He looked surprised, then put his own arm around me. Neighbour-woman looked surprised too, or maybe amused: maybe she thought *she'd* been doing him the favour. She took the hint, though, and drifted away.

Hey, you, I said.

Heya. What's up? He'd definitely not stuck to the alcohol-free stuff: his words were slurring.

What's Jason's Islamic name? I said.

You what? my husband said.

The name he took, I said, when he converted. Reverted. To Islam. When he married Aisha.

Oh, that, my husband said. Yeah, I don't know, he said. Shall I ask him? Where is Jason? Why?

It doesn't matter, I said, I just wondered.

Aisha had told me once that her maternal relatives, back in Pakistan, did this thing where they'd change a child's name if the child was badly behaved, or kept getting in trouble. They'd change it officially, with a ceremony and everything. It usually worked: as if the new name came with a new energy, new potential, or as if you really could leave your old self behind. I thought of the time in secondary school I'd decided to go by my middle name but was too shy to actually tell people. I'd taken my husband's name when we got married, in an ironic-not-ironic way, though now all I thought was the dullness of being yet another *son of John*, whoever the original John had been. There was something, I thought, something maybe even heinous, about having a whole other name, personality, possibility, even, and not even bothering to use it.

My other half, we'd called each other, self-mockingly, for the first few years of our marriage, and I suddenly wanted him to call me that again, his other half, his better. I thought of the books that used to live on his bedside table, when he used to do things like go on retreats to sweat-lodges in, I don't know, the middle of *Kent*, that I used to tease him about. The sheer ridiculousness of a bunch of white IT boys sitting in a circle in a tepee, drumming. The books had said things about the Yakuts of Siberia believing that every shaman kept his soul, or one of them, incarnate in an animal carefully concealed from the world. The Samoyeds of Turukhansk having familiar spirits in the shape of wild boars, which they led round on magic belts. Now I thought that he had part of mine, or at least, he'd had it. We'd been each other's gift, not obligation; each other's secret power. I wanted that again. I wanted him to do his sweat-lodge things again, and for me not to take the piss. I thought if he did, too, if we could get there, if we could only get back to that place—

Are you ok? my husband said.

I took a breath. The room resolved itself around me.

The boys and Chloe will need their tea soon, I said.

The boys have eaten their body weight in gingerbread. And Chloe's fine. Sure it's Christmas!

Ok, I said.

Why, do you want to leave or something, or what?

It's not that I want to leave . . .

So what do you want to do? he said.

I want you to take me home, I said. I want us to love each other always. I want us to drink less, at Christmas parties and in general. I want us not to have ambiguous or half-hearted encounters with friends or their neighbours in rooms at parties. I want you to take me home right now and lay me down.

I will, he said. And we will, and we will, and we won't, and I will and I will.

Except that for some reason, I didn't, couldn't, say any of it.

Mother's Day

WE WERE MORE THAN THE SUM OF WHAT OUR PARENTS DID, or failed to do. We were not living plots dictated by our genetic code, or circumstance. There had to be more to us than that because, if not, there was no hope for any of us. I believed that, or told myself I did. But as I approached the age my mother had been, I started to feel a rising, choking panic.

It wasn't the feeling of growing old, exactly, though that had been a big thing for her. She used to make me check her hair for greys and tweeze them out; would stretch the skin around her eyes with her fingertips and despair at the beginnings of crow's feet. She'd hated my birthdays too – each year she'd say that having a daughter that age made her feel ancient, made her feel she'd wasted her life.

I didn't feel my own life was wasted. But I did feel it was getting smaller and smaller. As if some part of me was dwindling.

Johann and I tried to rationalise it away. My working life had been on hold since our second baby was born, and then had come Covid. We were a family of four in a one-and-a-half-bed flat, and lockdown had intensified just how difficult that was – nowhere for the boys to let off steam, permanent chaos, it was no wonder I was on edge so much of the time. We needed a new chapter, Johann said – a fresh start.

He was clear, practical, focused – I admired those qualities in him. I wanted him to be right. So we sold our flat in Bow and offered on a house in a village in Essex. He works at the Crick Institute, studying genomic approaches to DNA damage repair: he would be gone in the mornings by six, not back till after eight at night, but we would have a whole house with almost half an acre of land by way of a garden, and the ancient forests of Hatfield and Epping nearby.

For me, forests just conjured the memory of trudging through Belvoir Park every Sunday on a nature walk, my dad, Ronan then me, never seeing any nature, just the slimy trunks of trees and fallen leaves. But Johann was increasingly into all that – he had his Level 1 Forest School qualification, which he'd gained at the weekends in Tower Hamlets Cemetery Park, and was working towards his Levels 2 and 3, after which he'd be able to teach Forest School himself.

I knew I needed to work out what I was going to do now. Through all of my teenage years and in my twenties I'd been adamant that I would never have children – how could I risk it? Because of this, or maybe in spite of it, I'd worked as a nanny and then at a playgroup. I'd loved the little ones. I loved how earnest they were, how open – how they lived entirely in each moment. Whatever they felt, they'd feel it with their entire bodies – they'd be wreathed in smiles or racked with sobs, and at hometime they'd hurtle towards the person collecting them as if they'd never been so happy to see anyone, ever. Those years had been healing: therapeutic enough that I had felt able to have babies of my own. But now it seemed nonsensical for me to go back to work looking after other people's toddlers whilst paying someone to look after mine.

Our offer was accepted. Our flat was all the boys had ever known. We talked to them enthusiastically about living in the countryside. About having a garden, a play-room, and one day a bedroom each. Our younger son was happy-go-lucky, he'd adapt. But our elder son was physic-ally timid, acutely sensitive to the moods of others, slow to feel at ease in a new place. When he outgrew a pair of shoes he wept, even when we bought him exactly the same pair of shoes again, until through his frantic hiccupping sobs we understood that he was crying for the old shoes and how lonely they'd be. His night terrors were so con-suming that I sometimes wondered, with guilt, if he was possessed – overwhelmed by feelings or fears not his own, because what could he possibly have to be so petrified about?

We moved at the very end of August, just in time for the new school year. Rudy started at his new school, going in every day in his little red jumper and a tight, brave face. The school had a nursery, so in a year's time Oscar would be able join him. In the meantime, he and I spent our days clearing the tangle of undergrowth from the garden. I pulled armfuls of weeds, prised broken bricks from the ground, hacked at ivy, and he trotted and clambered after me in his bright-pink all-in-ones, which had belonged to Rudy before him, and before that my best friend's daughter. They were covered in rainbows and unicorns, and he loved them. They were getting too small now, already – how had that happened so fast? You responded to their needs in such an urgent, numbing sort of present tense, then you looked up one day and years had somehow passed. I kept on telling myself that I should be treasuring this time, these high-skied September days.

At the back of the garden were thickets of brambles grown nine feet high, stems broader than my wrists, and along the sides were leggy roses neglected for years. I looked up online how to care for roses, but the first link I clicked on was all about how there's nothing less attractive than roses allowed to run away with themselves, and I didn't like its disapproving tone, so I just left them, and I left most of the brambles too, in case there were birds or other creatures depending on them. I wasn't sure what else to do then. I'd never had a garden before.

When the weather turned and the autumn rains set in, and it was too wet to go outside even in waterproofs, Oscar and I curled up on the sofa and watched episode after episode of *Peppa Pig*. The hill on it always made me feel dizzy – the cars would drive right up it and the children run headlong down, as if they didn't realise the danger they were in. But I loved the way Oscar laughed at it. His body fitted perfectly into mine, whatever way we shaped ourselves. It wasn't so long ago, of course, that he'd been part of me. Johann had told me that every foetus sends volleys of cells into its mother – at a certain point in the first trimester they cross the placenta, travel through her blood and lodge in various tissues, breast, thyroid, even brain. The phenomenon is called 'foetal microchimerism', after the hybrid animal of Greek mythology. The stem cells mimic the behaviour of the cells they find themselves around, and the interesting thing is that they are often found, and in greatest concentration, at sites of injury – C-section scars, breast tumours – as if they rush there to help with the defence, or the healing process.

But he said there was another theory too, that it isn't benign: maybe the cells' mission was to manipulate the body of the host to their advantage, producing more milk, say, or raising body temperature, despite the danger that overzealous cell division could cause cancer.

The push and pull of it – your body cannibalised itself to feed your children, but you had to nourish yourself too, and how to get the balance right?

I could still hear my mother's voice occasionally – not the things she'd said, but the tone of it, reading us stories, singing. But only in unguarded moments, and never when

I tried to. When I listened too hard, the voice would seem to break down, to snag on basic vocabulary – whether she'd said 'settee' or 'sofa'. I'd spent so much time away from home now that my own accent was almost gone too. Sometimes, speaking to someone here in the village, they'd ask me where I was from and I'd suddenly seem to hear myself from the outside, and wonder whose voice I was talking in.

Johann was worried I was too much alone in the house all day, these darkening days. We were sitting on the rug in front of the fire, and he said it so casually I knew he must have thought about it a lot. I didn't reply immediately; for a while we just both watched the flames.

I suddenly thought that I would love a glass of red wine – I thought of the way I might hold it up against the firelight, and the way the flames would light it up, make it jewel-like. But Johann didn't drink at all, and nor did I, these days.

'It's not that I'm lonely,' I eventually said.

There was no way of explaining to him how full the days actually were – the tedious mayhem of it all. The triumphs and tempests of looking after a four- and a two-year-old always sounded so petty, so banal – none of it translated to an adult who was working in the city, with other adults. When I described my day, it did sound lonely.

'I wish I could help you more,' he said.

'You do help,' I said. 'You do practically everything at the weekends.' I was wilfully misunderstanding him, and he frowned, but said no more.

And maybe, I thought, the loneliness was its own sort of insulation, a buffer. Since having the boys I'd felt, not the outrage or anger I expected towards my mother, but a strange sort of compassion for her – I felt it, and didn't know what to do with it. Sometimes it tipped into something akin to understanding: there were days when I was so terrified that I, too, would leave my boys that I almost wanted to do it, just so it was done, and it would be as much as I could do to pull the tangle of my thoughts back from there, from those places, and back into my own room, and time, and body – to my breath and to my heartbeat.

Rudy had a book that told you how many heartbeats different animals got in the course of a lifetime – elephant, mouse – as if they were weighed and packaged and distributed. He often asked me to work out, on my phone, how many heartbeats he'd had, I'd had, I had left. I worked along the biblical lines of three-score and ten, and the figures were reassuringly in the millions. But it did make you think – of sand in hourglasses, time slipping away from you. Of all the hopeless ways people in stories try to freeze or to reverse things.

After our mother left us, Ronan and I had spent hours lying under the rhododendron bush by the front gate debating what power we'd choose. She'd often despaired of our constant fighting, teasing, bickering. But our debates then were formal, polite. Ro almost always went for invisibility – the chance to creep up on people unannounced, to sneak in where you shouldn't, to get away with things. I often considered telepathy – the possibility of showing someone exactly how you were feeling – but almost always ended up going for flight. I imagined it would be cold, and not without effort – the air's uplift like the shock of diving underwater. You'd be exposed, up in the sky – buffeting winds, no cover from the rain. It was still what I'd choose. Neither of us ever went for time travel. Even if you could go back in time, I think, you couldn't change things, not really. You'd just have the added awful weight of the thing that was to come.

Christmas drew near. I suddenly wanted to see Ronan, and invited him to join us, though we barely talked these days. He worked at a Forbidden Planet in Birmingham, and from what I could gather it was his entire life. His latest thing, when we occasionally texted, was that all of our existence was a simulated reality – we were basically living in a computer game. He sent links to long Reddit threads proving that there were physics dilemmas better explained by a simulation than by a material hypothesis. If we were PCs, or playing characters, then it didn't matter what we did, he said, even kill ourselves, because we'd just be harvested back into the game. If we were NPCs, non-playing characters, then it mattered even less what we did because we weren't ultimately the ones doing it.

I wasn't sure which of his scenarios was bleaker. He had other theories too, that we were all just energy-generating battery cells for some big net of a matrix encircling the earth, but I'd never properly engaged with those. Sometimes I tried to ask him: did it matter to him whether or not things were 'real'? Because even if you *were* just animated bunches of someone else's pixels, did it change anything about the ways you lived your daily life? Didn't we each have to live our life, whatever we feared or believed, as if it mattered? Wasn't that enough reason – enough purpose – even just the flicker of possibility that it might?

Ronan didn't respond to my Christmas invitation for several days. When he did, he just said

why

I'd never invited him for Christmas before. I wrote several replies along the lines of *I'm 40 next birthday and have been thinking about the past, family is all that really matters, I'd like the boys to know their uncle,* and *I don't want you to be lonely,* all of which I deleted – they were far too senti-mental, Ro would run a mile from that sort of thing. In the end I replied

No reason, I'd just like to see you.

He said

> of course theres a reason
> is it because you want to talk about mum
> because i don't see there's anything to say

I told him that we didn't have to talk about our mother, if he didn't want to. But he just said

> you want to resurrect her
> do it by yourself
> im good tnx

On Christmas Day I sent pictures of the boys to my dad. He replied with little stone churches and palm trees, steep narrow alleyways and cobbled squares – he was on a cruise somewhere with Mandy. He'd married her when Ronan and I were both at university: and she was nice, I liked her well enough. She'd always said she'd never try to be my mother, and she didn't, she never did. My dad was elderly now – eighty-four. It wasn't fair to disturb his equilibrium, his final measure of happiness, by dredging up anything about my mother.

She had been much younger than our dad, by nearly twenty years. She wore ankle-length skirts and ruffled blouses that she bought from Fresh Garbage in town, with Doc Martens that she spray-painted silver. Her hair reached down to her waist and she kept it mainly in a plait that whipped around when she was excited or cross. Sometimes she wore purple lipstick, or lined her eyes in front of the hallway mirror with kohl that came in a little wooden pot with a tiny brush that she licked to a point. She'd been our dad's student – he taught evening classes in life drawing and portraiture – and she had wanted to be an artist too, only it turned out, she said, that she didn't have it in her. In the pictures of their wedding, which I used to pore over – his velvet suit and polka-dot cravat, her tight bodice with all the buttons – they were beaming at each other, and from the very first pictures of her with baby-me in a sling, then baby Ro – both of us naked in a washing-up basin while our mother, bubbles on her nose, laughs up at the camera – she looks devoted. Dad adored her. So did we. In the note she left she said that she was sorry, but we were better off without her.

I'd started second form that autumn, and Ronan went into the last year of primary school. He finished earlier than me, and he'd walk down to wait for me at the gates, sitting on his new backpack under the sycamore tree. His backpack annoyed me – it had come from a French mail-order catalogue, as had mine: one red with green trim, the other green with red, both with wide padded straps and matching lunchboxes that could Velcro on. Our mother had bought them that summer after reading about the dangers of lifelong neck pain from school bags. But how could you care so much about that, then do what she did?

I had ditched my backpack immediately, buying first a woven one from Dolcis, with thin leather straps that bit into my shoulder and which dog-eared all of my textbooks instantly, and then a black canvas messenger-style bag from the army surplus store that you could Tippex over with song lyrics. I tried to explain to Ronan that he needed a Head rucksack or a duffel bag, and in the meantime, at the very least, he shouldn't wear his red monstrosity on both shoulders. But he'd just blink up at me, and I'd try to suppress the urge to hit him. We'd walk to the library, grudgingly together, because it was better than going back home, and I'd listen to CDs from their collection, often the same one over and over until I knew it by heart, and Ronan would read. He got obsessed with riddles that year, which he discovered through Tolkien, and at teatime he'd quiz me and Dad on them endlessly – it had done my head in. I still remembered some of them now. *A wonder caught on water; wave become bone*: that was a lake iced over. *I am fire-fretted, and I flirt with wind; I am storm-stacked, and I strain to fly*: a log of wood chopped for the hearth.

A year or so later, Ronan got into *Dungeons & Dragons* and spent all his spare time in the arcade at the back of CastleCourt, druids and wizards and halflings, outwitting mind-flayers and storm-giants in other realms from which he never really returned. By then I was getting drunk after school and at weekends in the park on random concoctions of alcohol siphoned off or stolen from parents' drinks cabinets, or quarter-bottles of vodka or Buckfast begged from strangers going into the offy. Both of us had spent as little time at home as possible. Both of us had left as soon as we could, and never gone back. It was too late to try to bridge any of that distance now, with Ro or my dad: I'd known that, really.

Spring that year felt later than ever – or maybe the winter was just starker in the countryside, the bare trees, bare fields. It seemed impossible that it would come, until it did, and Johann reminded me that I felt the same way every year. I had planted bulbs around the back door, battling with a dowel to make holes in the cold, claggy earth, and though squirrels and mice had dug up and eaten a lot of them, there were still a few snowdrops and crocuses, then clumps of daffodils and narcissi, 'Fortune' and 'Tahiti' and 'Cheerfulness' and 'Camelot', flowers I'd chosen from catalogues for their names. There were enough to cut and bring some inside to put in jam jars, where you could sit and hear the papery buds crinkling as the flowers flexed before opening, slowly, then all at once, like a conjuring trick, I said to the boys, from a magician's wand.

I wanted them to remember that image. I wanted to instil in them the sense that the world is full of magic. To give them tools – possibilities – openings.

I turned forty. Here I was: exactly the age she'd been, and we were getting closer to what I always privately thought of as my mother's day. I started to have the recurring dream that plagues me at that time of year – every year since her death I've had it, without fail, and it builds in frequency and intensity until I wake up sweating, even screaming.

In the dream, I'm twelve again, and I'm in the museum – where my dad used to bring us, most weekends, for years. The museum's biggest attraction was, still is, a perfectly preserved Egyptian mummy named Takabuti. Her tiny darkened body, shrivelled to a sort of leather by the natron salts used to embalm it, lies taut and vigilant in its wooden qersu, one foot out of its bandages, as if ready to spring up. Her light-brown hair, elaborately coiffed, still holds its coils around her head, and although her eyeballs are long gone, her linen-packed eye sockets seem to stare at you through your own reflection in the Perspex box.

I was horrified by her – for a while obsessed with her. I would read every single placard in the room – about the funerary customs, about the embalming process, the after-life – even after I knew them by heart, putting off the inevitable moment when I'd have to look at her. It became a sort of game I'd play with myself: *I'm not going to look, I'm not going to look*, all the while knowing that I couldn't not.

And even more terrifying to me than Takabuti was the museum's second mummy, called Tjesmutperet. Like Takabuti, all of her major organs would have been extracted as soon as possible after death: most through incisions made in her left-hand side, and her brain tugged out in pieces through a hook inserted up the nasal passage. After preservation, each organ would have been wrapped in linen and replaced in its cavity, the body packed with sawdust then oiled and wrapped in hundreds of metres of linen, each layer sealed with warm resin. At every stage prayers would have been said to the gods of the cardinal points to aid her on her journey through the realms of the dead, at the end of which her heart would be weighed against a feather. If found to be pure, she would pass on into the Field of Reeds, the Field of Offerings, for ever and ever. But something had gone wrong for Tjesmutperet, in this world or the next: when she was unwrapped, her body had turned to black dust. Now here she and Takabuti lay, side by side, like some sort of morality tale whose meaning just eluded you.

It bewilders me now that my dad didn't see anything unhealthy in it, my weekly pilgrimages – almost against my own volition – to stare at the bodies of mummies, immediately after the loss of my own. But maybe he was just immured in the shock of his own bereavement.

I'm sure, had I told someone, they would have made the connection between my nightmares and my grief. But the dream was always too terrifying to articulate. It's hard to describe it even now, other than that it contains a long walk through corridors, and a mounting sense of dread, a cloud of black dust rises swirling, coalescing into the shape of a body, looming over me, eyes gaping, gaping mouth howling, and it is an effort to wrench myself away from there, to slam with a jolt back into my own body.

I know it's to do with my mother, but I've never known

what to do about it. It's ridiculous, I know, but every time a petition goes round online, to return ancient artefacts to the countries from where they were stolen, or looted, I sign it, in case that makes some sort of psychological difference – but it never does.

The nightmares that year were the worst they've ever been. The bleakness of the mornings – the feeling I'd been fighting endless battles in other realms – I was struggling to get up and to get Rudy to school on time, and the rest of the day feeling too thin-skinned to trust myself to function. Sleep deprivation does bring you close to a sort of psychosis, and I'd try to nap when Oscar did, but it wasn't enough. Johann and I were fighting, I was snapping at the boys. Rudy was wetting his bed. I felt in the grip of something that wasn't me, that wasn't mine, that was affecting all of us. Something fundamental needed to shift: something profound – as I had known, as I'd tried not to know – needed to change.

It was early summer by then, and the fields around us often smelled extravagantly of slurry. But the good days were beautiful – the rapeseed in full flower, such an extravagant yellow, the sort of yellow that feels like it's pouring from your solar plexus. On my mother's day, on a whim, I kept Rudy off school. I hadn't intended to – we were on our way there, and at the last minute I just didn't, couldn't bring myself to drop him off, to leave him out of my sight that day. Instead we kept driving, on through the countryside, at first at random, past the nearest village and the next, and then to a town where I knew there was a Friday antiques market.

There was a particular stall I remembered seeing there, a bric-a-brac table with old bottles and tarnished silver christening cups, tangles of old rosaries and cloak pins, brooches, everything jumbled up together. In a shoebox they'd had some strings of faience beads – tiny irregular tubes of terracotta, hundreds of them knotted together in elaborate patterns. I'd paused at them before, the child in me recalling all I knew of funerary rites and superstitions, the reverence with which they might have been wound round a mummy's neck. Now, I bought a string of them for the price the man was asking; I didn't even try to haggle. Back home we sat in the garden and I held them out, up to the sun.

'Once upon a time,' I said, 'these beads belonged to a mummy. This mummy is trapped, but we're going to free her.'

'Whose mummy?' said Rudy.

'No one's mummy,' I said, 'just *a* mummy. A mummy is—' But I stopped myself; that was guaranteed to give Rudy more nightmares. 'Never mind,' I said. 'The only thing you have to understand is that the mummy in the story was trapped.'

'How was she trapped?' said Rudy, frowning.

'She was stuck,' I said.

'Like in the mud?'

'Yes – why not. The mummy was stuck, but now we're going to set her free.'

'You're my mummy,' Oscar said, throwing his arms around my neck.

'Yes,' I said. 'Yes, I am – exactly.'

Then I tugged as hard as I could and broke the string. The force of it sent the beads flying in all directions, indistinguishable against the earth where they landed. There were a few remaining in my hand and I rubbed my palms together to free them. I knew some people would think it a dereliction – they'd been preserved for thousands of years, passed through dozens of hands, for this. I hoped it was worth it. I hoped that a symbolic act could also be real. If it couldn't, we were in Ronan's territory, where nothing could ever really matter or make any difference.

'I'm letting you go,' I said aloud. 'Look – I've done it. I'm setting us both free.'

I thought I might feel something then, but I didn't. The boys were bored already of my strange little game, running off and chasing each other, squabbling. I watched them for a while – it was hard to get the balance right, between when you should intervene and when you should just leave them.

And then I realised that several minutes had passed in which I hadn't thought of my mother. That sounds such a little thing, but it had never happened before, not on her day. I used to set aside the entire day to talk to her in my head – to be furious with her, or plead with her. Some years I'd be sure that wherever she was, she'd be thinking of me too – how could she not be? – and that somehow our thoughts would find each other. When I was pregnant for the first time I'd willed her to get in touch, to give me a sign – had been so convinced she would, it was a shock when she didn't. In subsequent years I'd tried to close off my mind to her completely, so that nothing would be able to get through, and the effort of that would leave me exhausted.

But for the first time, I was older than she had been. I was free, I told myself, to grow away from her now.

The summer passed. As August drew to a close, Johann thought we should have our own little ceremony, a celebration marking the first year of our new life. It was the sort of thing I normally shied away from – my mother had been into pagan things, corn dollies and St Brigid's crosses and Ogham stones. She'd always, I thought, been searching for something more, something else. That awful terror that she was wasting her life. But this was my life, I thought – this was what I got. So the boys and I collected blackberries from our brambles and made an apple-and-blackberry pie, baked a soda bread. We mixed up a jug of elderflower cordial with mint, took it all out into the garden and spread out a picnic rug. The skies were high and blue, the air still – the year poised at just that moment before it begins its descent, its tilt into winter.

'Well,' said Johann. 'This is our one-year anniversary.'

'What's an anniversary?' said Rudy.

'It's like the birthday of our coming here,' I said.

'Annus, year, and versus, turn,' Johann said. 'One year's circle around the sun.' He was quiet for a moment, and the boys looked up at him, expectant. For an awful moment, I thought he was going to cry.

'Hey,' I said. 'A whole year – we've done it. We really have.'

Johann rallied – shook his head and made a show for the boys of puffing out his cheeks and exhaling, then busied himself pouring and passing round cordial.

'To our new life,' he said, 'which is already just our life.'

We all touched cups. To our life, we said. To life.

After we'd eaten, the boys scampered round playing hide-and-seek. I thought how, when each of them was born and the midwife said, 'It's a boy', I'd been briefly, desperately sad I didn't have a daughter, and then very glad.

Johann and I wouldn't have any more babies. After Oscar, we'd given away all of the newborn paraphernalia, the clothes and Moses basket and car seat and bouncer. But we had started sleeping together again, and it was good. I had worried that we, that I, wouldn't get through this year, or wouldn't get further than it. But I had, we had, and maybe we were going to be ok.

It had passed, I thought: this year I'd dreaded more than any other. Though maybe time didn't pass – maybe it

234

stayed exactly where it was, every moment, and it was we who moved through it, each new cycle a chance again to get it right.

When the boys got tired, I sat them down beside me and showed them how to look for four-leaf clovers in the grass. Our dad had replaced our lawn with Astroturf, which gave you carpet burns when you fell, but was one less job for him to do. But before that, it had been a thick mass of clover. Every time we found a four-leafed one, we'd nip it by the stem and run with it to Mum, who pressed them between the pages of her heavy art books. They often came in clusters – where you found one, you were likely to find more. She was so delighted with each one we found that we'd sometimes search for hours in the hope of pleasing her. There'd been a knack to it – looking, but letting your eyes glaze over at the same time, running your fingertips over the leaves until one seemed to jump out at you. The luck was with us that day – within a few minutes, first Oscar, then Rudy had found one, and they shouted and laughed with joy.

Acknowledgements

ALL OF THESE STORIES OWE SO MUCH TO SO MANY, but certain stories owe particular debts of gratitude which I would like to acknowledge here. 'The Counting Sheep' and 'Daphne' were commissioned for broadcast by Michael Shannon, and recorded in Belfast for BBC Radio 4 – I am grateful to Michael, and to Louise Parker and Michelle Fairley, who first gave them voice. 'Lay Me Down' was given publication in the *Irish Times* magazine by Martin Doyle and Ciara Kenny in December 2022. 'Dark Matters' was commissioned by Ra Page and edited by Connie Potter and Rob Appleby for *Collision: Stories from the Science of CERN* (Comma Press, 2023). 'If You Lived Here You'd Be Home By Now' draws on the experience of Dr Kim Caldwell in Sydney during Covid times. 'Openings' owes a heartfelt thanks to Amna Jatoi for a long walk one rainy London evening discussing Sufi mysticism – and for the Pakistani food. The psychic as well as the physical space of 'Unter den Linden' was shared by Nick Laird and Glenn Patterson, and the conversations over those extraordinary days will long be with me. 'Cuddies' owes thanks to Yan Ge, for one conversation in particular; and another conversation with Yan, this time with Jill Crawford and Nadia Davids as well, unlocked something for me in 'Mother's Day'. And finally, also for 'Mother's Day', my respect and thankfulness to E. M. Forster, to Christopher Isherwood, and, for all it might mean, to Tjesmutperet.

I would also like to thank Joe Thomas for reading and responding to early, and often multiple, drafts with his characteristic flair, sharp advice and encouragement.

Most importantly, every single story here owes so much to my editor Angus Cargill at Faber – it continues to be one of the greatest privileges of my writing life to work in the way we work. Angus, thank you. Thank you to Silvia Crompton, whose care and instincts I value so highly and have come to rely on. Thank you to all those at Faber who have worked on this collection, from production to publicity, Josephine Salverda to Josh Smith, Ian Critchley for the proofreading, and thank you to Jack Smyth for the stunning cover design. Thank you, as ever, to Peter Straus at Rogers, Coleridge and White. And a very special thank you to David Torrans and all at No Alibis Press and bookshop, a beating heart of Botanic, and Belfast, and beyond.

Finally, my deepest thanks to Tom, to whom this collection is dedicated; and to William and Orla (and Zola!), such beautiful measures of our days.